Mystery of Mordach Castle

Weekly Reader Book Club presents

Mystery of Mordach Castle

WILLIAM MacKELLAR

ILLUSTRATED BY JERRY LAZARE

FOLLETT PUBLISHING COMPANY

CHICAGO

also by WILLIAM MacKELLAR

MOUND
MENACE

ISBN 0-695-80084-1   Trade binding
ISBN 0-695-40084-3   Titan binding

Library of Congress Catalog Card Number: 72-89578

Weekly Reader Book Club Edition

For Laurie

CHAPTER 1

THIS WAS MacDonald country.

This had always been MacDonald country. For centuries, the mighty Clan MacDonald, Lord of the Isles, had claimed this land. The name was on a hundred tombstones in the churchyard of Kenmore. Most of the stones were old and gentled with time. The words were a smooth faintness. Some words had faded into nothingness. Yet one word, defiant of time itself, stood out boldly from the rest. Stone after stone carried it like a banner:

MacDonald—MacDonald—MacDonald

His name was Duncan MacDonald.

He ran swiftly, his bare feet slipping easily through the bracken and coarse heather. Far down the flanks of the mountain, he could see the tiny huddle of gray-slated houses that was the village of Kenmore. Thin plumes of smoke drifted lazily upwards from the chimney pots.

His brown legs pulsed with strength. He could feel the flow of it within him. Oh, and it was grand to be the finest runner in all Kenmore. For he *was* the finest runner. He knew it. Yes, and this year he would be old enough to compete in the Kenmore Highland Games. The whole countryside would know then that no one was as fleet of foot as Duncan MacDonald.

The air, keen with the scent of far-off pine trees, stung his nostrils. The wind broke against his face in a long wave of coolness, and there was no end to it. The feel of the grass on the soles of his feet was like no other feeling in all the world.

It must have been like this in the old days, he thought, as his legs churned effortlessly over the rough hillside above the glen. How often Uncle Alec had told him of how the swiftest runner in each small village had carried the news to the next village. Usually, if the news were of war or other threats, the runner carried a fiery wooden cross to warn of the danger at hand. Perhaps had he, Duncan MacDonald, lived in those stirring times, his might have been the stout arm that would have passed on the fiery cross to the next clansman.

Suddenly, he crested a small brae and stopped, his heart thumping as he gazed at the scene high above him. It was strange how always his heart seemed to thump, even when he was not running, when his eyes fell on the massive ruin that was Mordach Castle, perched on its precipice above the Atlantic. Long ago, before most of its great walls had crumbled into a heap of weed-snarled stone, Mordach Castle had been the ancestral home of the Chief of Clan Campbell. Now the Campbells, the old enemies of the MacDonalds, were gone from the glen, the wild skirls of their pipes silenced forever, their fierce swords gathering rust against the damp walls of the castle.

But it was not only memories of the dreaded Campbells that quickened Duncan's heartbeat. It was something more. The knowledge that Mordach Castle was haunted by a ghost. The ghost of Mary Ellen. Everyone in Kenmore knew the story. How, long ago, Mary Ellen, a young girl from

England, had spent a summer at Mordach Castle. While there, she had fallen in love with Malcolm, the dark-eyed son of the Chief of Clan Campbell. A few weeks before the marriage, she had gone to a neighboring town to arrange for her trousseau. When she returned, it was to find Mordach Castle a smoking ruin after a MacDonald raid. Heartbroken, yet certain that somehow her Malcolm was still alive and would return, she moved into the deserted castle. There she lived by herself for the rest of her life, staring out at the Atlantic and waiting for her lover to return. It was shortly after she died that the whispers started. How on moonless nights the ghost of Mary Ellen walked the ramparts of Mordach Castle, a lantern in her hand to guide her Malcolm home. No less faithful to him in death than she had been to him in life.

Duncan stared up at the blackened ruin. Some there were, of course, like the minister and the schoolmaster, who smiled at the old story—but not many. Certainly not Duncan. Why, had not Uncle Alec himself seen the ghost of Mary Ellen, and it a long whiteness staring out into the blackness of the Atlantic? True, Uncle Alec's eyes were not as sharp as they once were, but he could hardly have been mistaken about seeing a ghost. Duncan nodded to himself, remembering. Yes, a place like Mordach Castle with its memories of old wars and old ghosts was best left alone.

He turned abruptly away from the nettle-choked path that wound upwards to the castle. Perhaps it was the knowledge that he was leaving dreaded Mordach Castle behind him that brought a new power to his legs as he rushed homewards. He was a good half mile away from the old ruin and well into Glen Appin when he heard it. A series of thin rasping sounds, as though a bow were being scraped harshly against strings.

He stood quite still. It was crazy. Why should anyone be out alone in the emptiness of Glen Appin playing a fiddle? It must have been the wind he had heard. The wind blowing up-glen and teasing a white hawthorne bush nearby. He nodded to himself, reassured, and smiled. Of course. Nerves. It all came from thinking too much about Mordach Castle. He suddenly threw back his head and laughed.

"Sh—sh!"

Duncan almost jumped out of his skin when he heard the sound. He jerked his head wildly to the right. Then to the left.

But as far as the eye could see nothing stirred in the vast emptiness of Glen Appin but the wind in a white hawthorne bush.

CHAPTER 2

"OVER HERE, Duncan MacDonald."

It was a hoarse whisper, and it came from back of a huge boulder. So did the mane of unkempt white hair. So did the aged brown face that looked like nothing so much as a shrunken winter apple. Duncan felt the air in his lungs go soft with relief. He watched as the skinny little man pulled himself from behind the rock. A fiddle as scarred and mottled by time as its owner jutted out from under a fleshless arm.

"Murdo," the boy exclaimed as he recognized the old man. Nobody knew Murdo's last name, or if he ever had one. To every farmer and sheep herder along the lonely stretches of Glen Appin, he was simply Old Murdo the Fiddler. The bow that he scraped across the strings earned him the few shillings he needed. "Annie Laurie" was the only tune Old Murdo ever played. Some said it was the only tune he *could* play. Old Murdo didn't mind. Regardless of the event for which he played, whether for funeral or fair, the tune that wheezed out of his ancient fiddle was always the same: "Annie Laurie."

"*Sh—sh!*" The old man pressed a warning finger to his lips and glanced around fearfully. Then with the hand that held the fiddle, he beckoned the boy towards him.

Duncan stared. Maybe Old Murdo was getting a little touched in the head as some of the villagers claimed. The boy looked over his shoulder. Nowhere in all Glen Appin was there a sign of life. Puzzled, he followed his feet to where Old Murdo stood next to the rock.

"Duncan MacDonald!" the fiddler burst out in a shocked voice. "Were you not minding at all where you were standing just now?"

Duncan looked back at the gentle, grass-covered swell in the ground. He frowned. There seemed little about it to distinguish it from the rest of Glen Appin.

"Croc an t-Sithein!" the old man exclaimed. "The hill of the fairies! You were standing right on top of their home!"

"I was?" inquired Duncan doubtfully. Again he looked back at the innocent little knoll.

"Aye, you were. That's why I was playing my fiddle. My father always said it was a clever one who kept on the right side of the wee folk. And if you want proof that they like the music, Duncan MacDonald, have you ever met one that didn't like 'Annie Laurie'?"

Duncan scratched his head. Old Murdo had a point there. Still— Again the boy's brows pinched in a frown. "You really believe, Murdo, the wee folk live down under the hill?"

Old Murdo shook his head pityingly. "And where else would they be living, boy, but under the likes of a hill? You will not be expecting now to find them biding in a house and they only three inches from toe to crown?"

"Mm." Murdo had a point there. More than a

few in the village thought Murdo a little crazy, but Duncan knew better. Murdo just looked at things differently. He said carefully, so as not to offend his friend, "There are some in Kenmore who no longer believe in the fairies, Murdo."

The old man sighed and nodded. "That will be true, boy, and more's the pity. Aye, but there was once a crofter named Tam Gunn, and he did not believe in the fairies either, and look what happened to Tam Gunn."

"And what did happen to him, Murdo?"

"It all took place a long time ago. Now it was not, mind you, that Tam Gunn did not *believe* in the fairies. Tam had too much Scots' sense for that. It was just that Tam never had a good word for them. He would go around wearing a green jacket with mother of pearl buttons, too, and himself knowing how jealous the wee folk are of anyone who dresses as they do."

Duncan nodded sympathetically. Any human being who went around with a green jacket and mother of pearl buttons was certainly looking for trouble.

"And what happened to him, Murdo?"

16

"One day Tam told his wife he was going out to one of the fairy hills to have sport with the wee folk. His wife waited up for him that night, his supper on the table, but Tam Gunn was never seen again by mortal man. All that they ever found was his green jacket cut into a hundred pieces and his mother of pearl buttons scattered around a fairy hill. That is why, Duncan MacDonald, it is well not to laugh at the wee folks."

The boy felt his face grow warm. "But, Murdo, I would not be thinking of laughing at them," he protested hastily.

"That is good. Even the new minister, I am certain, will not be laughing at them. Mr. Cameron has the good Highland blood in him and is a grand reader of books, besides being a minister. Well the same one knows that the fairies are fallen angels and not to be trifled with."

Duncan nodded in hasty agreement. Ian Cameron, the youthful minister who had just taken over the pulpit of the Free Church in Kenmore, was his friend, and if Mr. Cameron with all his university learning could be tolerant about the wee folks under the *Croc an t-Sithein,* then so could he, Duncan

MacDonald. True, there were some villagers who thought the young minister was too tolerant about a number of things. And not just the wee folks beneath the fairy hill. All this talk about understanding one another and forgiving your enemies. After all, as Uncle Alec said, if you went around forgiving your enemies you would soon have none left to forgive. A fine state of affairs that would be.

Old Murdo closed his eyes and sawed a few strains of "Annie Laurie" from his fiddle. He bowed gravely in the direction of the fairy hill as though acknowledging applause, then turned to the boy.

"And yourself, Duncan MacDonald, what brings you to Glen Appin?"

"I was at the running, Murdo."

"And why now?"

"Oh and I was just remembering the old days and the fiery cross."

Murdo said quietly, "The old days are best forgotten."

"That is true, Murdo, only my Uncle Alec says—"

Duncan was interrupted by a harsh scrape of

18

the bow across the strings. He said quickly, to change a subject that plainly upset the old man, "Is there anything new on all this talk about smuggling, Murdo? It was on the radio this morning that the police think the stuff may be coming in through some little Highland port on the Atlantic. Why just think, Murdo, that could be Kenmore!"

Murdo grunted. "I heard about it. Smuggling indeed! And around Kenmore no less. What now would anyone want to smuggle out of Kenmore?"

Duncan frowned. "But they're not smuggling it out, Murdo. They're smuggling it in."

"Smuggling it in?" Murdo exclaimed. "And that would be crazy now, and sinful besides. Has not the good Lord Himself given Kenmore everything it needs? What more would it be needing than what the Lord hasn't already provided, Duncan MacDonald?"

The boy scratched his head. Why was it always so hard to argue with the old fiddler? The good Lord *had* been kind to Kenmore. Where else in Scotland was there better grazing for the sheep? Or where were there more wonderful salmon than in the streams back of the glen? And if God had not loved Kenmore so much, why had He lavished such beauty upon it? Was any scene, anywhere, more lovely than the mists rising from behind Loch Doune and the mountains sliding in a great greenness into the black waters of the lake? No, as Old Murdo said, the good Lord had indeed been kind to Kenmore.

"There was another reason I was running, Murdo," he said after a long moment. "It will only be a month to the Kenmore Highland Games." He paused, then said matter-of-factly, "As you know, I'm a grand runner."

"You are that." Murdo thrust his hand deep into his ragged tartan jacket. After a moment, he brought it forth again, a small square of dusty yellow cheese between his fingers. He slid the cheese between his toothless gums without looking at the boy. "I do hear that this young Alan Campbell is a grand runner, too."

"Alan who?"

"Alan Campbell."

Duncan stared. "But there are no Campbells around Glen Appin, Murdo, as well you know."

"There are now." He smiled slyly with his heavy-lidded eyes. "Tinkers. A family of them. Up at the head of the glen."

"Tinkers!" Duncan repeated scornfully. Lower even than the Gypsies who came each spring to Glen Appin were the tinkers with their flat carts and their little knock-kneed Highland ponies. A tinker was bad enough, but a tinker who was also a Campbell, that was even worse. Duncan felt his face harden.

"You would think would you not, Murdo, that any Campbell would not dare set foot in the glen after all the things they have done to the Mac-Donalds and others."

Old Murdo looked off into space. He said mildly, "The old days are gone."

Duncan controlled with an effort the angry words that threatened to spill from his lips. Too often he had heard from Uncle Alec about the treachery of the Clan Campbell. Too often he had heard how they had massacred the MacDonald men, women, and children in the Pass of Glencoe. Yes, and after being taken into the MacDonald home for two weeks and treated as friends besides. Uncle Alec would not soon forget the perfidy of the Campbells. Neither would Duncan.

He said slowly, choosing with care the words that crowded his tongue, "So he is a grand runner then, this Alan Campbell?"

"He is that. A grand runner like yourself. I saw him only yesterday in the glen. Running like a deer he was."

Again Duncan bit back the words that rushed to his lips. Yes, a tinker would be running. No doubt from the police if the stories could be believed. It was no accident that every year when they came, there was a rash of missing chickens around the village. And this one was a Campbell! How he feared and despised the name. The sun was warm against his face, yet he could feel the sudden chill in the air. It was the wind from the north. The wind blowing from the head of the glen where the Campbells were.

It was strange how in the old days they had always struck from the north. There had been a saying then. A saying that had been born after one such dark foray by the treacherous Campbells.

There never came any good thing out of the the north but a cold wind in autumn.

Duncan MacDonald felt the sudden coldness again. The coldness that came from the head of Glen Appin.

CHAPTER 3

HE LEFT Old Murdo to his fiddling and headed homewards. He ran more swiftly than before, for now he was the bearer of news, like the couriers of the fiery cross that he had been thinking about only a few moments ago. Uncle Alec, for one, would be furious when he learned that the Campbells were back in the glen. Uncle Alec had a long memory. None of that let bygones-be-bygones nonsense about him. No, Uncle Alec wasn't like Mr. Cameron.

The sky suddenly darkened, and he increased his pace. Now he could make out in the distance the small whitewashed cottage with the gray slate roof that was his home. Ever since that day when his father's boat had gone down in Loch Doune, Duncan and his sister, Fiona, had lived with Uncle Alec. Their mother had died when they were very small. Perhaps the fact that Gavin MacDonald's death had taken place so near to the old Campbell castle had added to Duncan's fear of the grim ruin. Be that as it may, no one could have been kinder than Uncle Alec, although Duncan was aware that many in Kenmore found the hot-tempered little man a source of some amusement. Actually Uncle Alec was his great uncle, having been his father's uncle.

A quick flurry of rain stung his cheeks like suddenly tossed pebbles. It stopped as suddenly as it started, and the sun swam free from the net of a black cloud that had snared it. In an instant, the shadows lifted, and the whole glen and the brooding hills seemed to rise upwards in a soundless explosion of color.

A few minutes later, as Duncan drew near to the village, he glanced down and saw someone kneeling in the small garden at the rear of their cottage. Fiona of course. Fiona was a year younger than he was, and a good runner too. For a girl, that was. She also knew how to twist Uncle Alec around her finger. Duncan waved and Fiona, holding a wicker basket of string beans in one hand, waved back. The knowledge that his sister was watching made him lengthen his stride. Three minutes later, he was in the small vegetable patch. She listened quietly as Duncan told of his meeting with Old Murdo.

"Campbells?" Fiona's green eyes were thoughtful. "And tinkers too. Uncle Alec will be wild when you tell him."

Duncan jerked his head in quick approval. "Uncle Alec knows the Campbells for what they are."

The girl shook her head. "Poor Uncle Alec. What good does it do to go around forever talking about all those old feuds and battles? The minister—"

"The minister?" Duncan interrupted. "And what does Mr. Cameron know of the treachery of the Campbells? Granted he's clever enough about the Pharisees in the Bible. But the Pharisees are not the Campbells. Besides don't forget, Fiona Mac-

Donald, that Mr. Cameron is a minister. It's his *job* to love everybody."

Fiona smiled. "So Mr. Cameron is only doing his job. Maybe if some of us did ours half as well as he does his, Kenmore would be a lot better place than it is."

He choked on the rush of words that leaped to his throat. That was the trouble with trying to reason with girls like Fiona MacDonald. You never seemed to get anyplace. He breathed hard and gazed at her with bitter eyes. "And you a MacDonald! You'd better not let Uncle Alec hear that talk, my fine lady. He'll tell you a thing or two about the Campbells."

"But that was all so long ago, Duncan. Everything's changed now."

"The Campbells don't change!" he cried fiercely. "Never!"

"Well then," she exclaimed with a toss of her head, "let's hope we do. Besides I've got more to do than worry about the Campbells."

He said nothing. What was there to say? He looked gloomily around the diked garden. "Where's Wullie?"

"Wullie?" she laughed. "Sleeping most likely. A lazier dog in all Scotland you will not find than our Wullie, bless him."

"It's the laughing stock he is of Kenmore," he said. "All the big lazy brute does is eat and sleep. Even when I go for a walk with him, the old faker gets tired."

"Maybe he's just smart. Anyway, if anything ever happened to our Wullie, it's sad you would be yourself, Duncan. There's not another dog like him."

"That will be true enough," he said with a grunt. "He's a rare one all right is lazy Wullie." He pretended a scowl of annoyance. He knew Fiona was right though. Fat and lazy Wullie might be. Fatter and lazier than any dog in the whole of Glen Appin. Yet what other dog could do the things that Wullie could do? Could take any day and make it a brighter one by just being in it? Maybe Wullie didn't know any of the tricks that smart dogs are supposed to know. Yet one trick he did have. The trick of stealing his way into your heart when you weren't looking. And Wullie, once in your heart, was just too lazy to move out again.

The sound of voices must have awakened the animal. A long freckled nose gently nudged open the kitchen door. An immense dog waddled into view and lumbered heavily over to the boy. He gave him a swipe of his huge red tongue. He moved his tail twice, first to the left, then to the right. Finally, apparently exhausted from his labors, he curled himself up in a huge brown heap and closed his eyes in sleep.

The boy grinned as he followed Fiona into the kitchen. "At least Wullie never gets into any trouble. He's just too lazy—"

He never finished the sentence. There was a loud *bang* as the door slammed shut. Duncan spun around and stared at the round little man with the huge white moustache. The fierce blue eyes seemed to be doing a Highland reel above the pink cheeks. With a bound, the little man was across the room and had seized a huge broadsword from the wall. He waved it about.

"Uncle Alec!" exclaimed Duncan. "Are you all right?"

"Campbells!" thundered Uncle Alec. "At the top of the glen! A whole cartload of them! *Och*

and the sheer impertinence of them! After all that they did to us at Glencoe in 1692. But they'll not catch *this* MacDonald asleep in his bed. Come one, come all!" He lunged wildly with his great sword. Duncan, by skipping smartly, just got out of the way.

"Uncle Alec!" he cried. "It's me! Duncan!"

His uncle paused, his chest heaving, his pink cheeks glistening with sweat. "Have no fear, lad. We'll sell ourselves dearly. To the battlements!"

"Now, now, Uncle Alec," Fiona said quietly, "well you know there's no reason at all to carry on so. Duncan was saying they're just tinkers—"

"Tinkers!" muttered Uncle Alec. "On top of everything else, tinkers!" Mumbling, still protesting, he let the girl lead him over to his armchair on the right side of the fireplace. She brushed her lips against his brow and took away the sword. "A cup of tea and a bannoch with cheese. Now sit yourself down here and don't worry about anything."

The little man glowered into the flames leaping up the chimney. "It's not just myself I'm worrying about, Fiona," he said finally, all the fire gone from his voice. "It's Duncan here."

The boy stared. "Me? And why should you be worried about me?"

"Are you not a grand runner, boy?"

"I am."

"And is your name on the list for the Kenmore Games?"

"It is." Would Uncle Alec never get to the point?

"There's another name been added to the list. I just saw it outside the post office."

Duncan knew the answer deep inside him before his lips framed the question.

"And what name would that be, Uncle Alec?"

"Campbell. Alan Campbell."

CHAPTER 4

DUNCAN FORCED a matter-of-fact tone to his voice. "So there will be one more to beat in the race," he shrugged.

"Only this one is a Campbell." His uncle took a noisy sip of his tea and shook his head morosely. "They're treacherous, the Campbells. Mark my word he'll find a way to beat you, boy. A sly way. A cunning way."

"Please, Uncle Alec," Fiona began before her uncle stilled her with a majestic sweep of his arm.

"The trouble with you, girl, as with so many others like you, including the new minister—respect him as I do—is that you don't understand at all the nature of the Campbells. It was not for nothing that they were feared and hated by every other Highland clan. Who was it caused the MacGregors to be outlawed? The Campbells. Who was it caused Bonnie Prince Charlie to lose his chance for the crowns of Scotland and England? The Campbells. And let us not forget what they did to our own MacDonalds that fearful night in the Pass of Glencoe." He shook his head and fixed his eyes on his nephew. "That is why I tell you, boy, be careful."

Duncan nodded. He did not have to be reminded of the evils of the Campbells. "I'll be careful, Uncle Alec," he vowed.

Fiona opened her mouth to say something, then apparently thinking better of it, closed it. She stirred her tea, then after a long moment glanced across at her uncle. "Have you heard anything new on the smuggling, Uncle Alec? I heard some talk that there was an inspector up from Glasgow. They think perhaps the smugglers are using one of the small Highland ports."

If she had hoped to calm the round little man by changing the subject, she was mistaken. Uncle Alec was not the sort who calmed easily. A glitter leaped to his eyes, and he tugged angrily at one end of the fierce white moustache that swept from ear to ear across his round face. "It's the idiotic government!" he roared as though addressing a company of guards on parade. "Taxes! Taxes! If they'd only cut down on those taxes of theirs, there wouldn't be any reason to smuggle." His pink cheeks glowed. "If Bonnie Prince Charlie had only won in 1746, mark my words there would have been none of this taxing nonsense today. And why didn't he win? Because of the Campbells, that's why. It's because of *them* that we've got all this smuggling going on! Them and this idiotic government we've got in London!"

Duncan said, "It was on the radio this morning —about the government thinking that maybe the smuggling is being done through the West Highlands. Just as you were saying a minute ago, Fiona. That would explain the reason for that inspector from Glasgow you heard about. They've probably got them checking on every little port around here." He suddenly grinned. "I don't think our Constable Lindsay will like it, having these Glasgow fellows ordering him about. He's a slow-moving man is

John Lindsay and not the kind at all that likes to be pushed around."

Fiona's green eyes snapped. "Isn't it exciting! Just suppose it was our own little Kenmore. Why we'd be in all the papers and on the television and everything."

If Uncle Alec had heard the exchange, he said nothing. His gaze was fixed on the twisting, spiraling flames in the fireplace. Slowly, as weariness tugged at his eyelids, they closed. For several moments, he dozed, his breathing soft. Suddenly with a quick start, his eyes opened and he swung his head back. He looked guiltily around him, as a guard would who had fallen asleep while on duty. For a moment his glance touched the great broadsword, then seemingly reassured, his head fell slowly forward on his chest. The next moment he was sound asleep.

Fiona looked at him, smiled, then crossed over to the window. She stared out into the great emptiness of Glen Appin. "And why shouldn't it be Kenmore, Duncan?" she asked softly. "I mean if I were a smuggler, I'd pick a place like Kenmore. It's small. It's out of the way. It's right on the Atlantic.

And once across Glen Appin, it's only a few miles to a highway going to Glasgow. Oh, Duncan, wouldn't it be wonderful if it was Kenmore? Why we'd be famous!"

Carried away by her enthusiasm, Duncan was almost on the point of expressing quick agreement when prudence bade him hold his tongue. No sense in encouraging her. After all, Fiona was like the rest of the girls around Kenmore. If they said something and you agreed with it, they thought right away they were as clever as you were. Cleverer, maybe, because they had thought of it first.

"That, Fiona MacDonald, is as it may be," he said airily.

At least she couldn't disagree with that.

It was strange. Two weeks had passed since the Campbell family had moved into the glen, yet not once had Duncan seen any of them in Kenmore. Normally when the tinkers came, they were all over the village. The women would hawk their cheap trays and baskets from door to door, while the men, quick-eyed and smooth-tongued, would be earning a shilling here, and a shilling there.

Duncan found himself frowning. More and more, he was anxious to see this Alan Campbell. Especially now that he knew he would be running against him in the Kenmore Games. Quite obviously, this particular tinker kept to himself, although some member of his family had entered Alan's name in the race. Perhaps the reason that the Campbells did not come into the village often was because they were after the mushrooms. Duncan nodded to himself. He had heard that the wild mushroom trade in Scotland was run by the Gypsies and tinkers. Wild mushrooms sold for nineteen shillings a pound in the big cities. A tinker who knew where the good beds lay could earn quite a bit of money. There was also a nice shilling to be made selling white heather to the tourists in Edinburgh. For some reason, the tourists believed that white heather was lucky and would bring them good fortune. There was white heather hidden away in the hills beyond Glen Appin. Maybe that was where these Campbells were right now. Yet for a reason Duncan could not have explained, he was strangely unconvinced. Why was this Alan Campbell keeping to himself?

Duncan finished his chores around the cottage and after picking up the weekly paper in the village for Uncle Alec set off on the homeward trip. Although he could easily have jogged all the way without breaking stride, he stopped when he came to the coarse moor grass that swept down through the encroaching heather in a dark green channel. So many thoughts kept turning and twisting in his mind. Perhaps if he rested for a moment in the grass, he would be able to sort out the thoughts in his crowded head.

Hardly panting from his run, he let himself down on the grass facing the glen. He drew his knees up under his chin and craned forward. It was a good position if one wanted to think. The knees pressed firmly under the chin kept the head rigid. He had laughed a little when Old Murdo had given him the secret. He did not laugh any longer. Old Murdo had been right. When a man's head was held level and firm, the thoughts didn't seem to tumble around inside so easily. Murdo also claimed that the reason the world was in such a mess today was that nobody sat still anymore. And though others might laugh behind Murdo's back, Duncan was not so sure but that the old man wasn't right. After all, if all those generals and politicians just stood still, how could they possibly get themselves into so much trouble?

In the distance, Duncan could see the great ruin that was Mordach Castle. Without any conscious effort on his part, his eyes quickly slid away from the grim pile of blackened, fire-scourged stone. He stared away to the left—to the endless sweep of the Atlantic. The gray of the ocean flowed into the gray of the sky so that Duncan could not tell where the one began and the other ended. How long he stared he would never know. When he finally turned away, he saw the figure of an old man plodding through the thick grass. Duncan's face lit up when he noticed the fiddle under the scrawny arm. He let out a wild "Hullo, Murdo! Up here."

The old fiddler stopped, cocking his head like a suddenly startled bird. Finally, after peering all around him, he spied the boy. He raised his bow in greeting. Duncan scrambled down the rough slope until he came to where the old man waited.

"Murdo, where have you been hiding yourself? I haven't seen you for ages."

Murdo chuckled. Or at least he seemed to be chuckling, for the loose skin around his sunken gums quivered, and a rasping sound struggled up from somewhere deep in his chest. "Oh, and I've been here and there, Duncan MacDonald."

"Yes, but more there than here," protested the boy, pleased to see his old friend again.

Murdo closed one eye in a slow wink. "A man can only be in one place at one time, eh lad?"

"That will be so, Murdo. Only somehow the place where I was was never the same place you were."

"That is because there are so many places."

Duncan darted a quick glance at the fiddler. Quite plainly something was on his mind. The boy drew his brows together in a broad show of concentration. One did not ask direct questions of Old Murdo at times like this. That is if one expected direct answers. One played little games with the fiddler. Old Murdo liked games.

"That is right, Murdo. The world is full of places."

Murdo winked again. "And so is Glen Appin. That is full of places, too."

"That is so, Murdo, Glen Appin is full of places. And it was in one of the places in Glen Appin that you have been?"

"It was. A place where you do not go. A place where few in Kenmore go."

Duncan sighed. Sometimes it was hard to play these little games with Murdo. Like now for instance. Glen Appin was full of places that he, Duncan, never visited. He could spend the rest of the day guessing.

"I give up, Murdo. Where is this place?"

Old Murdo looked crestfallen. "But you have not even tried to guess, boy." He paused, then peered craftily at Duncan. "I will give you a hint. A castle is a place, is it not?"

"That is so, Murdo. Only there is only one castle in Glen Appin, Mordach Castle. And no one goes there." He paused. "You will not be telling me that you yourself have been there, Murdo?"

The fiddler popped a square of yellow cheese between his toothless gums. "Not exactly *in* the castle, boy, but near it. In fact, just outside it." His jaws rotated. Quite plainly, the old fiddler was enjoying himself.

"Then that is why I did not see you, Murdo. There is something about Mordach Castle that I do not like. Maybe it's the old stories about the castle itself. Maybe it's the ghost that's supposed to walk there at night, the ghost of Mary Ellen. Maybe it's just that the place itself gives me the shivers. No, Murdo, you would not be likely to see anyone from Kenmore around Mordach Castle."

"That is true," said the old man gently. "But I saw someone. Someone who does not live in Kenmore."

Duncan stared. "You saw someone there? Outside Mordach Castle?"

"I did. A little way from the castle."

"Someone who doesn't live in Kenmore?"

Old Murdo nodded, pleased. "Give up?"

"I give up, Murdo," the boy exclaimed impatiently. "Who was it?"

Murdo laid a skinny finger alongside his nose. "Young Alan Campbell, the tinker's son."

"Alan Campbell? But what would he be doing near Mordach Castle?"

Murdo smoothed the long white hair that spilled over his shoulders. "That I will not be knowing."

"But it is strange, that," mused Duncan. "No one goes near Mordach Castle."

"The tinker's son does," Murdo pointed out.

"Perhaps he has not heard about the ghost of Mary Ellen. About how she walks on the ramparts of the castle to guide young Malcolm home."

Murdo cocked his head and considered the suggestion. "He is a Campbell. The same as young Malcolm was himself. No, I am sure he has heard the old story."

Duncan frowned. "Perhaps there are mushrooms near the castle. The tinkers know where all the good mushroom beds are."

"That is so, Duncan MacDonald," Murdo agreed. Again he slid a small piece of cheese into his mouth. "Only there will not be many mushrooms a boy will be finding at midnight."

"At midnight?" exclaimed Duncan in astonishment.

"At midnight. You see sometimes when sleep will not come at all, I take a walk through the glen. I will not be remembering why that night I should find myself a short way from Mordach Castle. It was a dark night, mind you, and the moon only

44

peeping out once in a while from behind the clouds."
He paused to munch on his cheese.

"And then?" urged Duncan. Would the old
fiddler never get to the point?

"All at once I heard quick footsteps, as though
someone was running across dry leaves. It was dark,
but I stood behind a rowan tree and waited. Just
that moment the moon came out. Then I saw him.
He ran past just six feet from where I was hiding.
It was the tinker's son."

"But why, Murdo?" was all Duncan could say.
"Why should he be going there at midnight?"

"Your guess, boy, will be no worse than mine."
The old man tightened the strings on his fiddle.
"Oh, and who can say? Maybe it was that the lad
was just curious about the ghost of Mary Ellen.
After all, was not Mordach Castle the old home of
the Campbells?"

"But why should he be running, Murdo?" the
boy persisted.

"You ask too many questions. Anyway, Old
Murdo has other things to think about than why a
tinker's son should take the path to Mordach Castle.
Am I not right, Duncan MacDonald?"

The boy did not answer. He looked off into the distance where Mordach Castle, with all its bloodshed and heartbreak and mystery, stood silhouetted against the western sky. It looked like nothing so much as a long black cobra, poised to strike. Duncan felt the sudden coldness of sweat against his ribs.

"You are right, Murdo," he said finally, "you are right."

His troubled eyes were still fixed on Mordach Castle.

CHAPTER 5

WHY HAD Alan Campbell gone to Mordach Castle at midnight?

All the way home, the question kept tugging at the coattails of Duncan's mind, pleading for an answer. Yet no matter how he struggled to come up with a logical reason for the mysterious visit, he was still groping for an answer when he spotted the cyclist approaching along the dusty trail from the village.

"Mr. Cameron!" he cried, when he finally recognized the youthful figure in the gray suit. "It's yourself."

The minister braked to a halt and slid off the

bicycle. "As you say, Duncan," he said pleasantly, "it's myself." He drew the back of his hand across the sweat that peppered his brow. "A little warm today."

The boy smiled. He liked the Reverend Ian Cameron. He knew though that some of the more proper members of the church frowned on the fact that he insisted on making his pastoral calls on a bicycle.

"Yes," Duncan said, "it is a bit warm today, Mr. Cameron. Uncle Alec says the weather's been changing lately, what with all those rockets and the Americans walking around on the moon as though it was Glen Appin. Uncle Alec says if God had wanted men to walk on the moon, he would have said so in the Bible."

The minister smiled then nodded. "I see what he means, Duncan. Still I don't remember that God said anything about riding bicycles either." His gray eyes twinkled. "Maybe you'd better not tell your Uncle Alec you saw me. Sometimes I'm not quite sure he approves of me as it is."

"Why now, and Uncle Alec likes most everybody," Duncan replied. Suddenly aware he hadn't meant to say it just that way he added hastily, "I mean although he likes most everybody, he likes some people better than others." He felt his face go warm. "*You* know what I mean, Mr. Cameron," he said lamely.

"Of course I do, Duncan." The minister clapped him on the shoulder and put his foot on the pedal. "Well, I suppose I should be getting along. There are some strangers in the glen, I hear. I promised I'd get over to see them today."

"Strangers in the glen?" Duncan frowned. "You will not be meaning the tinkers, Mr. Cameron?"

"They *are* tinkers I believe." What might have been a smile bent the minister's lips at the corners. He looked away idly. "They tell me they have a boy about your age."

Duncan stiffened and backed away warily from the trap. Mr. Cameron didn't know the Campbells the way that Uncle Alec and a lot of other people in Kenmore knew them.

"That is so, Mr. Cameron," he said. "He's in the race, I hear." He paused, then said, "I'll be seeing him at the Games."

49

The minister's eyes touched the boy. He nodded and pushed the bicycle forward. "That's right. You will be seeing him then. Well, good-bye, Duncan. I'll have to be on my way."

"Good-bye, Mr. Cameron." He stared after the retreating figure on the bicycle until it vanished behind a bend in the path. He had been surprised to learn that the minister was going out of his way to call on the tinkers. Uncle Alec and some of the others would not like it when they heard about it, and they Campbells to make matters worse. Besides, the tinkers had set up their camp away off in the north end of the glen, well outside what most people would have felt were the parish limits. But then maybe Mr. Cameron had a different idea of how far his parish extended.

Young ministers sometimes had queer ideas about things like that.

"I don't understand it at all," Duncan said that afternoon to Fiona. "What was this Alan Campbell doing around Mordach Castle? And at midnight, no less."

"It is odd," she admitted after a long moment. "Old Murdo, he could not have made a mistake, could he?"

Duncan shook his head impatiently. That was the trouble with girls. You always seemed to have to tell them the same thing twice. "Of course Murdo saw him! And after all, he rushed past only a few feet from where Murdo was hiding. Besides the moon was shining right on him. Murdo may be old, but even Uncle Alec says he's got the youngest eyes in all of Glen Appin."

"I suppose you're right, Duncan," she conceded reluctantly. "Still, they live in a tent. Maybe, like Old Murdo, he couldn't sleep and just felt like taking a walk."

"You don't believe that, do you, Fiona MacDonald?"

She looked away unhappily. "No, I'm afraid I don't."

"Besides, if he feels like walking so much, why doesn't he walk down to the village now and then? Why only to places like Mordach Castle?" He suddenly thought of something. "You don't think it might have something to do with all this smuggling that's been going on?"

"Why, Duncan MacDonald, what a thing to say. Simply because his name is Campbell, and he's a tinker."

He felt the hotness under his cheeks. His voice carried a little too loudly to his ears. "I didn't mean it that way, as well you know. I just wondered why anybody should be sneaking around Mordach Castle at midnight. Nobody in Kenmore would think of going near the place. And you will remember that most of this smuggling talk started *after* the tinkers arrived in the glen. Maybe there's no connection. I'm just wondering, that's all."

"Why not ask him?" she said mischievously. "That would be the easiest way to find out what he was doing."

He shook his head angrily. What was there about dreaded Mordach Castle that had brought Alan Campbell there? And why had he been running? The fact that he had gone at midnight could only mean it involved something he did not want known. There was, of course, another way of possibly finding out. A way that made the blood quicken in his veins at the very thought of it. To go to Mordach Castle by night, as Alan Campbell had done.

The idea, once planted in his mind, was impossible to uproot. There was no place that he feared more than Mordach Castle. It was from there that the Campbells had set out in the old days to pillage and burn. Yes, and it was in Mordach Castle that the ghost of Mary Ellen, lantern in hand, waited for her lover to return. That is, if the old story was to be believed. And who did not believe it? Too many had seen her lantern flickering in the night. Too many had heard her sobbing when the moon was full. Yet, fear Mordach Castle as he did, he would still go there. As Alan Campbell had gone. Alone and at night.

He turned to his sister. "You will keep a still tongue in your head, Fiona," he admonished sternly. "Tonight I will go up by the castle to find out what is going on there. There will be a full moon. If there will be anything to see, I will see it." He paused and looked over at the slumbering figure by the fireplace. "You will mind not to say anything to

Uncle Alec. He would only get excited and think the Campbells were back in the castle. Then he would want to lead an attack with this big sword of his. So you will say nothing. You understand, Fiona?"

"Not a word, Duncan," she breathed. "The old castle at midnight? It will be our secret—yours and mine."

He didn't quite like the way she had put it. His eyes narrowed. "None of your tricks, my fine lady. Just remember to keep your mouth shut."

"Not a word, Duncan," she promised again, her hands clasped in front of her. "Do you really think we will see anything up there?"

"No, I—" he began before he bit back on the words he was about to speak. He fairly glowered at her. "And what do you mean by 'we,' Fiona Mac-Donald? This is a job for a man. Besides you might get hurt."

"Do you really think so, Duncan? I mean that I might get hurt up by the castle?" Her eyes fairly danced in her head. "Wouldn't that be exciting though?"

He scowled at her in wrath and despair. If ever

he was to take a firm stand with this uppity sister of his it was now. He took a deep, deep breath.

"Fiona MacDonald," he enunciated with slow deliberation. "You will understand one thing. Mordach Castle is no place for a girl. I'm not saying there's a ghost up there, mind you. Still if there was, you would be off like a rabbit."

"Like a rabbit," she agreed, a little too quickly to his liking. "I'm a fast runner too, only not as fast as you are, Duncan."

"I didn't mean it that way," he returned angrily. "It would not be me who would be running, it would be you, Fiona."

"Oh, I see."

"Anyway, the whole idea is plain crazy. A girl—no! And one that can hardly run any faster than Wullie!"

"I can run as fast as a rabbit," she pointed out. "You just said so."

"Oh and will you shut up!" he said, looking over at where Uncle Alec slept, his head slumped on his chest. "Just you mind what I'm telling you. You stay here tonight with Uncle Alec while I find out what's going on up at Mordach Castle."

She said sweetly, "That's too bad."

Something in the way she said it made him pause. "And what's too bad?"

"Nothing. It's just that if I was with you, Duncan, I would not be here."

"Now don't you start any of Old Murdo's games with me. Of course if you weren't here you would have to be somewhere else."

"And if I were somewhere else, Uncle Alec couldn't ask me where you were."

"Uncle Alec will be sleeping."

"Maybe." Her eyes were all innocence. "But if he heard a noise he might wake up."

"What kind of noise?"

"Oh the usual kind of noise, Duncan. Maybe I might fall out of bed or something."

"You might at that," he said, bitterness thick in his voice.

"And don't you see, Duncan, what might happen? If I *did* fall out of bed, and he *did* hear me, he *might* ask me where you were? And of course I'd just have to tell him. So that's why I've got to be with you. Then there won't be any chance that I'll fall out of bed."

"I hope the next time you do you break your neck, Fiona MacDonald," he hissed. "And if anything happens to you tonight, don't blame me."

"What time?" she whispered.

He gritted his teeth. "After bedtime." It was enough to make a man weep.

"I hope something happens!" She clapped her hands softly together in excitement. "Do you think something will really happen, Duncan?"

He glared at her. "Not if you stay out of my reach, Fiona MacDonald."

Oh, and why had the good Lord ever made little sisters?

CHAPTER 6

THE WHOLE evening had taken an eternity to pass. Would Uncle Alec never put away that old book on the Scottish clans and go to bed? It seemed that ages had passed before Duncan, his nerves raw with tension, finally heard a creaking from the bed in the next room. Ten minutes later, Uncle Alec's nasal breathing, deep and rhythmic, carried to the boy's impatient ears.

He waited for more than two minutes to be sure his uncle was asleep, before signaling to Fiona. Never in all his life had he felt more guilty about anything. With Fiona at his heels, he eased back the lock on the door. It hurt him to be sneaking out behind the old gentleman's back. Despite his fiery temper, Uncle Alec had always been open and fair with him. They had never kept any secrets from each other. Until now, Duncan reminded himself grimly. Yet how could he have told him he was going to Mordach Castle? Uncle Alec would have leaped at once for his broadsword. Then with a shout of *Fraoch Eilean,* the ancient battle slogan of the MacDonalds, he would have set out to do battle with the Clan Campbell.

Slowly, under the gentle pressure of Duncan's hand, the door swung open. Suddenly Duncan heard a slight sigh. He froze, his breath a thickness in his throat. Then understanding came.

"Wullie!" he whispered between set teeth. He stood rigid. Who would have thought the laziest brute in all Glen Appin would be awake at this hour? It was crazy. Wullie must have thought so too. After making himself more comfortable in his big box by the fireplace, he made no further sound.

"He's asleep," Fiona whispered in Duncan's ear after a long pause. Quickly they slid through the door. Duncan drew it silently behind him, then followed Fiona soundlessly up the gravel path from the cottage.

The moon played hide-and-seek in a long, wispy cloud. Duncan, picking his way carefully across the glen, was grateful for the moments of darkness. He knew this particular part of the country like the back of his hand. There was no need for the brightness that seemed to twist the rocks into odd human shapes and to tease the mind with vague questions.

The wind was cold and keen with the scent of meadow-sweet and distant clover. To his straining ears came the endless croon of brook water passing over hidden rocks. Despite the sting in the air, he could feel his face warm and moist with a faint sweat. The closer they drew to the massive pile of dark stone that was Mordach Castle, the quicker his heart seemed to pump. From somewhere to the left, a dog barked twice, then was still.

Duncan halted when they arrived at an open field of scree and broken rock. He did not like the idea of crossing it in the brightness of the moon. It was completely barren, without a bush or a tree anywhere. It was a fairly narrow channel of broken stone that extended both right and left. Anyone watching from the heights of Mordach Castle could scarcely fail to observe an intruder crossing it. Perhaps the Campbells had created it long ago as an additional protection for Mordach Castle. In any event, it had to be crossed now. It was the only direct route he knew that would bring them to the castle, unless one could climb up the sheer rock face from the Atlantic.

Duncan hesitated. It was too bright out there. Too empty. He bit his lip. If Fiona had not been with him, he might have turned back. Only he couldn't turn back now. He could almost sense the eyes watching from the shadows around Mordach Castle. From somewhere in the tough moor grass in which they lay concealed, he could hear Fiona's breathing, soft and quick.

For nearly ten minutes, they lay and stared at the channel of rock and chipped stone that lay like a protective moat below the castle. In the brilliance of the yellow light, the scene was as sharply etched and clear as though the sun and not the moon were shining.

Duncan's nerve ends were beginning to fester. There was a queer dryness in his throat too. Suddenly, just when he was on the point of giving up, he noticed it. A slender wisp of black cloud drifting towards the edge of the moon. Fiona must have noticed it too, for her fingers pressed against his arm. He watched as the cloud slid over the moon, as the blackness slid across the deserted scene in front of them.

"Now!" he whispered, scrambling to his feet. Head low, he fairly charged across the scree, with Fiona only a few feet behind him. From the breadth of the cloud, he had calculated they would have no more than fifteen seconds to cross. Fifteen seconds to get to the shelter of the trees that hid the trail that wound up the steep incline to the castle. Fifteen seconds before the moon would swim clear and bathe the whole scene in brilliant light. Fifteen seconds. Would it be enough? He knew it would be enough for him, the best runner in Kenmore, but would it be enough for Fiona?

"Hurry, Fiona," he urged. He slowed up, grabbed her arm, and propelled her forward. Now they were twenty yards away from the beckoning path in the trees. Now ten. The moon was almost free. Desperately, he thrust Fiona forward as the light started to sweep like a great silver scythe across the open field. Then suddenly under his feet he felt it. Heather! They were across!

Sanctuary gained, he darted with relief up the old trail, a few steps ahead of Fiona. All at once, he felt his right foot strike hard against something. His ankle jerked upwards violently. The ground seemed to rise up out of the night with lightning speed. The next instant, he was spread-eagled on a carpet of dry pine needles and withered bracken.

He lay quite still. He could feel, with a quick intensity, the pain that licked at his right ankle with a hot, dry tongue. Suddenly there was a scurry of footsteps.

"Duncan! Duncan, are you all right?"

He nodded, afraid to trust his voice. With Fiona's arm for support, he struggled to his feet. He set his teeth against the pain when his injured foot touched the ground.

"At least it's not broken, Duncan," she said, an edge of relief in her voice, "but I'm afraid you won't be doing much running at the Kenmore Games."

A tide of despair welled up deep inside him. The same thought had just crossed his own mind. To have won the race at the Kenmore Games would have been the most wonderful thing that had ever happened to him. But there would be no winning it now. Not with an ankle like this.

He did not protest when she took his arm and helped him back down the trail they had just entered. There was no point now of continuing on to Mordach Castle. He barely remembered Fiona getting him back across the open rock field.

He could have wept. Here he was, the fastest runner in Kenmore, and his little sister had to help him along. It was too much for any man, far less one with the name of MacDonald. The only comfort was that Fiona was a MacDonald too.

He was on the point of thanking her for her help when he bit back the words. No, it would not be wise at all to admit he had needed her a few moments ago. It would just go to her head. Girls were like that. Especially Highland girls. Still he had to say *something*. He chose the words carefully. "You are not a bad runner, Fiona MacDonald," he said grudgingly. "No, not bad at all."

He caught her quick smile, then looked hurriedly away. Nothing more was said all the way home until they were about two hundred yards from the cottage. Suddenly he stopped, the question that had been vaguely teasing the edges of his mind for the last half hour, firmly secured.

"Fiona, I—I never trip like that. I'm quick on my feet, as well you know. And yet I fell over that old root or whatever it was back there." He shook his head. "I don't understand at all."

She said softly, all the mischief gone from her voice, "Perhaps, Duncan, you would understand better if you knew it wasn't a root you tripped over."

"It wasn't? Are you sure?"

"Yes. I went over and saw it for myself while you were sitting up looking at your ankle."

He stared at her. "And if it wasn't a root I tripped over, Fiona MacDonald, what was it?"

"A wire, Duncan. A wire stretched between two trees."

CHAPTER 7

HE WHISTLED between his teeth. "So someone placed it there! Just high enough to trip over."

"But why, Duncan?"

"Why?" He shrugged. "Most likely an alarm of some kind. That trail is the most direct way up to the castle. A prowler coming up the trail as I did would trip the alarm. Anyone waiting up by the castle would be warned that someone was coming up the old trail. When the alarm wasn't needed, it could simply be unhooked. Yes, that's the way it was, most likely."

She nodded slowly, as though convinced against her own reasoning. "Do you think maybe it had something to do with all this smuggling talk?"

"Maybe."

"Yes, maybe. And maybe not."

"But somebody had to put the wire there, Fiona. And nobody in Kenmore, as well you know, goes near Mordach Castle. So whoever did it, didn't come from Kenmore." Despite the pain that coursed through his leg, he could feel a quick beat of excitement deep inside him. "So that's why I think it could have something to do with the smuggling." He paused, then said grimly, "There is just one thing that bothers me, Fiona."

"There is?"

"What Alan Campbell, the tinker's son, was doing the other night near the Mordach Castle."

Old Murdo studied the swollen ankle. Murdo was clever with bones. There was none in Kenmore could set a broken wrist or a dislocated shoulder like Murdo. Men said it was a gift, and Murdo did not argue the point.

"It is a sprain just," he muttered. "It is the lucky one you are that it was not broken."

"Yes," said Duncan dispiritedly. Since last night, he had been doing a lot of thinking. And it wasn't pleasant thinking. The Games were only two weeks away. It would be a miracle if he would be able to enter the race, far less win it. Already the ankle was swollen and discolored. For the past six months, all his thoughts had been of one thing only—the race that would climax the Kenmore Highland Games. The race in which he, Duncan MacDonald, would show his heels to the fleetest runners in all Glen Appin. And now, not only could he not run, he could scarcely walk. He had never felt quite so miserable.

Old Murdo, his brown face creased and trenched with the lines of age, lifted his head and regarded the boy. "Aye, it is easy to know what is on that mind of yours, Duncan MacDonald, 'Here I am the fastest runner in Kenmore, and Old Murdo could give me a head start and beat me if he had a mind to.' You will learn, boy, that sorrow is no less a part of life than pleasure. Aye, maybe more, I'm thinking."

Duncan could not answer. How could this old man understand the bitterness that stretched his heart? How could he know what it meant to have one's dreams blotted out in the twinkling of an eye?

How could he, so infirm of foot, realize the anguish that was Duncan's at that moment?

The fiddler must have been reading his thoughts, for he grunted to himself. "You will be thinking, most likely, that Old Murdo does not understand. He that is a relic just and all the warm blood dried up in him. But well I can remember when these legs were no less strong than yours, Duncan MacDonald. When no foot was fleeter in the heather than mine. Fast as the wind I was. Aye faster, for many's the time I raced it across the glen." He paused and winked. "And will you believe it, boy? When Murdo got to the other side and turned around, why there was the wind just catching up with him."

Duncan smiled. "You were a grand runner too then, Murdo, like myself?"

"I was."

The boy watched as the old man dipped the long strips of linen into the bubbling spring water, then pressed them against the swelling. Miraculously the ice-cold compresses stilled the pain that had throbbed through his ankle.

"Why it feels better already," he marveled.

Old Murdo grunted. "Do not be thinking you

will be at the running tomorrow, boy. No, nor for a while just."

"But I will be all right for the race, won't I, Murdo?" he cried, a new excitement in his voice. "Why it feels good as new already."

Murdo did not look at him. It was as though the old fiddler had not even heard him. "You will bathe it every two hours," he said gruffly. "And you will mind and rest the leg."

"Of course, Murdo," Duncan agreed impatiently. "But the race! I *will* be able to run in two weeks, won't I?" Just a few short moments ago, he had been certain his ankle would never have healed in time for the Games. But it was different now. Everything was different since Murdo had treated the injury. It was easily seen why everyone agreed that Old Murdo had the cleverest hands in Kenmore.

Murdo did not look up. He was silent as he wound the broad cravat expertly under the boy's foot and around the ankle. Only when he was finished did he lift his eyes. He spoke deliberately, slowly.

"You are right, boy. If you mind me, the ankle

should be well enough. Well enough at least for you to enter the race. Only—" He did not finish the sentence.

"Only what, Murdo?" prodded Duncan.

"Only I'm wondering if it will be well enough for you to win it."

CHAPTER 8

"IT WAS a Campbell trick!" thundered Uncle Alec the next morning as he brought his blackthorn walking stick down hard on the kitchen floor. "Are you blind, boy, that you are not seeing that at all?"

"But—" Duncan began before Uncle Alec smote the floor again.

"Away with you! Oh the cunning of it! All of the Campbells are cunning!"

"The Campbells?" Duncan frowned. He knew of course that they were cunning just as Uncle Alec said. But what could they possibly have to do with his injured ankle? He was beginning to regret having told him about his injury. Still, how could he have concealed it? Besides, he loved Uncle Alec despite his fiery temper. How could he have gone on deceiving him?

"The Campbells," intoned his uncle. "Those tinkers at the head of the glen. They were the ones who did it, I am telling you. They are sly fellows all of them." Grumbling under his breath, he helped himself to a bowl of brose and fresh cream.

"The tinkers? You mean Alan Campbell? The one that is in the race?"

"Aye, that one, I'm certain sure of it. He must have seen Old Murdo watching him that night near the castle. He must have learned Murdo was a friend of yours. Knowing that, he knew fine that Murdo would tell you. With his sly mind, he guessed you would wonder what a Campbell was doing outside Mordach Castle at midnight. And he guessed, too, you would come back to find out. He was waiting for you, boy, with his cunning wire trap. Like a hunter waiting with his snare for a rabbit."

Duncan could feel his mind reeling. "But how could he have known Murdo would be there to see him?"

Uncle Alec waved a hand impatiently and with

the other, he twirled one free end of his fierce moustache. "You ask too many questions, boy. While the MacDonalds dream, the Campbells scheme. But that it was a trap I know as well as I know my name's Alec MacDonald." He sipped his brose noisily, then reached for one of the griddle scones that Fiona had just baked.

"But why should he set a trap, Uncle Alec? Why should he want to do me harm?"

Uncle Alec seemed to hiss rather than speak the words as he leaned across the plain pine table. "Because the same one is a Campbell. Because you are in the race with him. Because he knows it is you, Duncan MacDonald, he must beat if he is going to win. That is why." He stopped and gazed triumphantly at his nephew. "And do not you see? He knew you would be running. You always run. He was sure you would go up the trail to reach the castle. Oh, and it was simple, just!"

Duncan nodded, convinced in spite of himself. "And he knew that no one in Kenmore would likely be near a place like Mordach Castle at night. Only myself, after listening to Murdo, would be coming along the old trail."

"That's how it was," said Uncle Alec darkly, "and now it will not be a MacDonald who will be the star of the Kenmore Games. It will be a Campbell."

"But it will not be that bad," Duncan protested. "Of course I have to take it easy for a bit. Still, Murdo thinks I should be able to enter the race." He could not find it in his heart to add what else Murdo had said. That he could now scarcely hope to win.

"Bah! How can you, with one leg, beat a lad with two?" He pushed himself heavily back from the table, crossed stiffly over to the hearth, and poked a thick black poker into the gleaming peats.

Duncan did not answer. He had been thinking the same thing himself. If what Murdo said were true, his ankle would not be fully mended by the time the Games took place. And if it was not fully mended, he could not win. Someone else would. Someone named Alan Campbell.

He stood quite still, letting the bitterness trickle along his veins. Perhaps it would be better if he withdrew his name from the race. Then he could simply shrug and say the result might have been different had he, Duncan MacDonald, been fit enough to run. The thought was no sooner in his mind than he dismissed it. Never! Better to run and lose than quit and make excuses.

"There's one thing I'm not understanding in all this," the boy said finally, "why nobody seems to see anything of this Alan Campbell. Where does he keep himself?"

Uncle Alec scowled. "He's a tinker. He knows how most people feel about tinkers and Gypsies. He will be knowing his kind are not welcome here in Kenmore."

Duncan felt uncomfortable. Somehow it did not seem altogether right. He did not like the tinkers any more than did any of the other villagers. Tinkers were dirty and lived with dogs and horses. The tinker men were often drunk and loud. And everyone knew tinkers, men, women, and children, were dishonest. Still, despite all of that, it hardly seemed fair that this Alan Campbell should feel he had to shun Kenmore.

Suddenly Duncan remembered his ankle. If what Uncle Alec said were true, it was that same Alan Campbell who had deliberately set out to injure him—to either put him out of the race or prevent him from winning it. No sense at all in feeling sorry for anyone like that. There was only one thought that continued to trouble him.

How could Alan Campbell have possibly known that he would meet Old Murdo outside Mordach Castle?

And if he had not known, then what *had* Alan Campbell been doing there at midnight?

CHAPTER 9

DUNCAN HAD been amazed at how well the ankle had healed under Old Murdo's care. Now, ten days later, he was trotting easily through the heather. True there was still a tenderness, especially if he put too much strain on the ankle. But on the whole, he was delighted at how well it had come around. Following Murdo's instructions, he had not run hard, but he felt certain he had not lost in any way his fleetness of foot.

Sometimes as he jogged over the glen, he took Wullie with him. The whole thing a joke though. At least to Wullie. Plainly, the dog had other and more rewarding things to do than to gallop aimlessly around Glen Appin. Things like resting for instance. Things like watching the wind as it played tenpins across the sky with little puffs of clouds. After waddling good naturedly after Duncan for about fifty yards, Wullie would call a halt to the whole foolish business. Most dogs make a small half turn before lying down. Not Wullie. It was too much work. Wullie simply collapsed in a furry heap wherever he was, like a big circus tent in a high wind. And Duncan could always be sure that Wullie would not have moved from that spot when he returned. That was another thing about lazy Wullie. You could trust him.

Leaving Wullie behind, the boy loped easily over the sparse yellow grasses and straggly clumps of purple-red heather. A mist sifted up from the bogs near Loch Doune, obscuring the young blue of the early summer sky and the dour, lumpy hills that encircled the glen. It started to rain, soft and small and insistent. He did not break stride, glad of the quick wetness that seemed to lean against his face. The whole glen was awash with gray now, all the bright colors drained away in the rain and the fog.

The sky was so low above his head that he had the feeling if he but stood on tiptoe and reached upwards, he could have touched it.

As quickly as it had started, the rain blew out to sea, and the mist lifted. As though a curtain had been lifted, Glen Appin heaved itself up from the gray void that had held it. Duncan stopped, transfixed by the glory of the pageant unrolling before him. There were some, mostly visitors, who thought the glen a stark and lonely place, treeless, cheerless, endless. A dark, forbidding place that pinched the heart and crushed the spirit. But not Duncan. It was only a question of knowing Glen Appin in her various moods. Like now.

He watched as the sun picked its way delicately across the heather-shaggy moorland and the swamps around Loch Doune. The waters of the lake, normally so dark and somber, flashed and shimmered in the pale light. From somewhere near at hand came the familiar scolding notes of a stonechat. It was a scene of peace and innocence.

Suddenly the sun swept across the marshes, and it was a scene of peace and innocence no longer. There, lifted in stark relief against the lime-red sky was Mordach Castle, its fierce turrets, its battlements, its blackened, fire-scourged walls. Duncan stared at the great heap of crumbling stone. Even in the brightness of day, the aura of death was there, clinging to the walls like the ribbon of ivy that clung to its east face above the Atlantic.

Then as Duncan watched, as soundlessly, as swiftly as it had vanished a moment ago, the mist swept back across the castle from the sea. In the twinkling of an eye they were gone, the fierce towers, the battlements, the blackened, fire-scourged walls.

Nothing was left in the all-enveloping mist. Nothing at all. Only the aura of death remained.

Only that.

CHAPTER 10

ON THE day before the Kenmore Games, the last of the carnival bunting was draped across High Street. Dozens of flags flapped in the breeze: the Union Jacks; the blue and white Saint Andrew's crosses; the yellow Lions Rampant of ancient Scotland. Freshly painted wooden stands ran the length of the village green. Tarpaulin-covered refreshment booths, each gaily pennanted, had already been set up. Duncan marveled as the workmen brought in great boxes of meat pies, rolls, ice cream, and pop. Never in all his life had he seen so much food and drink. But then never had he seen so many visitors crowding the streets of Kenmore as he had seen today. They were everywhere, all lured by the special magic of the Highland Games, the pageantry, the color, the contests.

The contests. He knew that the footrace in which he was entered was only a small part of the competitions that would be staged. There would be tugs of war. Hammer throwing. Bagpipe playing. Sword dancing. Caber tossing. Yes, and a hundred things besides. Yet as far as he, Duncan Mac-Donald, was concerned, there would be only one contest. The footrace in which he and Alan Campbell were entered.

It was baffling that he had yet to meet the tinker's son. Not once, either in the glen or the village had he laid eyes on him. He would have been almost ready to believe that there was no such person as Alan Campbell in all of Glen Appin had it not been for two things. Old Murdo had seen him. And his name was still on the list of runners for tomorrow's race.

Of course there was something else. Perhaps the stranger was not a strong runner at all. Perhaps he was no better than Tom Kerr or Will Johnstone or any of the others who would be in the race. Yet Murdo had seen him. What had the old fiddler said? "Running like a deer he was." Yes, that had been it. Murdo was not one to make a mistake about a thing like that. And after all Murdo had been a runner himself once. Had raced the wind across the glen. Aye, and had beaten it. Duncan felt the smile that nudged the tension from his face. Well, if Murdo could beat the wind across the glen, he, Duncan MacDonald, could beat this mysterious Alan Campbell. In a considerably better frame of mind than he had been a few minutes before, Duncan picked up the link sausages at the butcher's and set off for home.

He ran easily, still not completely trusting his leg. Although it no longer pained him, he had thought it wise not to put too great a strain on it unnecessarily. Time enough for that tomorrow when he would need all the power and the strength he could command. And if what Uncle Alec suspected had been true about the wire trap, it would be quite a surprise the same Alan Campbell would get when he saw Duncan MacDonald as fit as ever. Oh, and wasn't it going to be a wonderful day tomorrow!

A hundred thoughts crowded Duncan's head as he tugged the rough covers around him that night.

Soon all the thoughts would fade away. Soon sleep in a great gray mist would sweep over him. And when he awoke, it would be morning. Kenmore Games Day. The skirl of pipes and the beat of drums and a hundred flags snapping in the breeze above the crowds. His head on the pillow, he closed his eyes to more vividly capture the scene. Then between one breath and another the mist came in from the sea. Came in a great soundless tide and swept over him. As the mist from the Atlantic had swept over Mordach Castle.

And when the mist-tide went out, Duncan went with it. Out to a sleep as deep as the gray ocean itself, and all the waves hushed in a great stillness.

CHAPTER 11

DUNCAN AWAKENED at six. Perhaps it was the sound that had aroused him, small and insistent, it seemed to come from far away. It was a pleasant, soothing sound. Drip—drip—drip. Suddenly he leaped straight up in bed. No! Not that! Rain? On the day of the Kenmore Highland Games? It was too much to bear. With a cry of anguish, he rushed to the window. The rain had stopped, but the leaves, limp and sodden, still shed their moisture. The sky was slate gray, but in the east, behind the sagging sycamores, he could see slits of brilliant blue. And while he gazed, his heart sick with pleading, the sun broke through the overcast, and the wet leaves glowed in a soft, amber light. With a long sigh of relief, he swung the window open and drank in the fresh morning air. It was going to be a grand day for the Games.

Everyone was up early. Fiona was already pouring the porridge, and the warm steam was just beginning to rise in the kitchen when Duncan got there. Uncle Alec, usually a late riser, was making the tea. Even Wullie was astir. Caught up in the sudden activity, and no doubt wondering what all the excitement was about, he lurched through the house, getting in everyone's way.

Of course there was only one thing they talked about over the porridge and toast. The Games. Not so much the Games, though, as the race. Duncan's race. Duncan talked too, but not as much as the others. Somehow, as far as he was concerned, everything had been said that needed to be said. But not Uncle Alec. He was in a rare mood.

"Just wait!" he roared. "We'll show them, you and I. Remember, boy, there was no one as fleet of foot in the old days as the MacDonalds. It was always a MacDonald who was picked to race through the glen with the fiery cross when danger threatened. Always!"

"But—" the boy began before his uncle banished him into silence with a majestic sweep of his arm.

"But nothing!" He suddenly froze, a heaping spoonful of porridge suspended in midair. His fierce blue eyes gleamed craftily. "And those Campbells. Won't they be the surprised ones though when they see you in the race. And after that devilish trick they played on you up by the castle." The pink cheeks glowed over the white moustache. He laid down his spoon, then rolled his hands together gleefully. "Do you know something, Duncan? I have a feeling in my bones that this is going to be the grandest Highland Games we've ever had in Kenmore!"

"Please, Uncle Alec," Fiona remonstrated. "Your porridge is getting cold." For some reason, she had become unusually quiet during the last few minutes.

Duncan glanced quickly at her and grinned. He did not have to be told what was on Fiona's mind. He knew her too well.

"You will not be troubling yourself, Fiona Mac-Donald, about my ankle," he said airily. "It is as good now as it ever was. Maybe better, what with all the rest it's had and everything."

She nodded uncertainly, then picked up the tea-cups. The hint of a shadow still clouded her face as she removed the tartan tea cosy and poured the beverage.

Duncan shrugged good naturedly. No sense at all in trying to explain to the girl. No doubt she thought because he had been taking it easy that he did not have his old-time speed. He smiled to himself. Fiona would learn along with the others. Anyway, if she didn't know anything about running, she certainly knew how to make tea. He took a long sip. It was strong and dark, the way he liked it best, with plenty of sugar and a top-taste of peat smoke from the fire.

"I think you are right, Uncle Alec," he said finally. He could feel deep within him the slow beat of a gathering excitement. "It *is* going to be the grandest Highland Games ever."

Everything after that was confusion. A wild, colorful, heart-stopping, dizzying confusion. Marching feet and brave kilted bands. The straining muscles of the mighty caber tossers as they flung the great twenty-foot trees into the air. The shot-putting and the hammer throwing and the sword dancing and the Gaelic storytelling. The six-a-side football and the tug of war. The cheers from the packed stands as the brawny hockey players sent the ball screaming upfield from their vicious, crooked sticks. And over and above everything that was happening, the skirling, rising-and-falling, blood-tingling music of the restless pipers.

Suddenly Duncan felt a quick pressure on his arm. Uncle Alec pointed to the clock on the grandstand. "Only fifteen minutes more. I'm thinking you should be getting ready, boy."

Duncan stared. Why it couldn't be time for the race. It was impossible. Fifteen minutes? Why he must have been dreaming. He would hardly have time to change before the race started. With a cry of anguish, he squirmed his way through the dense crowd. How daft could he have been to have waited so long? After what seemed an eternity, he reached the dressing rooms at the rear of the stands and slipped into his running clothes. Only then did he pause to look around and greet the other youngsters who would be in the race with him. All of their faces were familiar to him: Tom Kerr, Hughie Watson, Dugal Grant. All that is except one. The dark, sensitive face of a youth who was sitting quietly apart from the others. Duncan did not have to be told who the stranger was.

The mysterious Alan Campbell.

CHAPTER 12

DUNCAN CROUCHED low, his shoulders tilted over his slightly parted fingers, his body tense. Two hundred yards away, on the other side of the track and at the far end of the grandstand, was the tape. He had drawn the outside lane, the one next to Alan Campbell. Not that it made any great difference which lane he drew, as the track was a staggered one because it was curved. In the strange silence before the pistol shot, he felt his skin crawl under the gaze of the watchful eyes of the packed stands. Uncle Alec's eyes would be there, too. And Fiona's. And Old Murdo's. All of them, right at this moment as he crouched, every nerve and muscle straining with tension. Was he not, as Uncle Alec had said so many times, the latest in the long tradition of MacDonald runners? He *had* to win.

All at once, the silence was shattered by the *crack* of the starting gun. His legs seemed to receive the message before his mind. With a bound, he was away from the starting block and into his sprint, his long legs churning rhythmically.

He had broken well, thanks to the tremendous leg power he had developed from his daily hill-running. He was in front now, well into his stride, his head high, his arms loose. He could hear, seemingly coming from miles away, the endless roar of the crowd. His feet fairly skimming across the ground, he leaned his body slightly into the turn at the end of the track. He had just swung smoothly into the homestretch when he heard it, a violent break in the rhythm of sound in his ears. It could mean only one thing. Someone behind him was coming up fast.

He dared not look behind him to see who it was. His legs flew faster. Then out of the corner of his eyes, he caught the edge of a shadow. There had been nothing there before. Only now it was no longer a shadow. It was Alan Campbell, thundering up the track to close the gap between them.

Duncan did not panic. He was too fine a runner for that. He knew precisely the power in his body, as a skilled auto racer knows the power in the engine of his car. And he knew the reserve that was there in his legs waiting for his mind to trigger it. The reserve he had hoped not to have to use that afternoon. Now with the tape only fifty yards away and Campbell threatening, Duncan swept into high gear.

He had always been a strong finisher, one with the proverbial kick that distinguished the top runners. Now, for the first time since the injury to his ankle, he called on the full force of his speed and stamina. Campbell had just inched past him to the roar of the crowd when Duncan made his move.

They were neck and neck now, elbows flailing, chests heaving, feet churning. A good ten yards to the rear was a fading Dugal Grant, with the rest of the field strung out behind him. There were only two runners in the race. Duncan MacDonald and the newcomer to Glen Appin, Alan Campbell. The roar of the crowd was ear-shattering as the two boys swept towards the tape, now only thirty yards away.

Suddenly, just as Duncan inched past Alan Campbell, he felt a quick stab of pain pierce his right ankle. Perhaps it had been a cinder snared in his shoe. Perhaps an unevenness on the ground. Or perhaps it was just that the ankle had given away under the stress placed upon it. Had not Old Murdo hinted at just such a possibility? That although his ankle might mend well enough for him to enter the race, it might not mend well enough for him to win it.

His breath came in wracked, torn gasps. With every contact his right foot made with the ground, fresh pain washed over him. There was a whirling confusion inside him as he tried desperately to flog his faltering legs forward. He could never finish the race now. Never. Campbell was far out in front, his arms outflung to breast the tape. Duncan's blurred vision picked up other forms whirling past him: Dugal Grant, Tom Kerr, Hughie Watson. His muscles sodden with fatigue and agony, he struggled after the others. He never remembered hobbling across the finish line. At least he had not quit.

He could have wept. He slumped forward on the bench near the stands, his damp head between his hands. The medals had been given and the pictures taken. The race was over. Now the crowd was astir with a new excitement as the bagpipers marched. No one took any notice of the boy on the bench.

"Sorry."

Duncan looked up when he heard the voice. He stared when he recognized the speaker.

Alan Campbell.

CHAPTER 13

THE LAST person Duncan had expected to see at that moment was the tinker's son from the head of the glen. He eyed him warily, suspiciously. What had brought *him* here?

"Sorry about what?"

"Your foot. Something happened to it. All of a sudden you stopped running." He paused and looked uncomfortable. "I don't like to win that way."

Duncan grunted, remembering everything Uncle Alec had told him about the Campbells. "And what way do you like to win?"

The tinker's son stared at him as though not quite understanding the question. "Well now, I like to win fairly. You were running a fine race. I'm sure you would have won it. Then just about thirty yards from the finish line something happened."

Duncan laughed without humor. "It didn't happen thirty yards from the finish line," he said bitterly. "It happened near Mordach Castle. When I tripped over a wire that somebody had rigged across the trail."

Something in the way he said it made the newcomer pause. He looked wonderingly at Duncan. When he spoke, it was haltingly. "I see. And you thought maybe because I'm a Campbell and a tinker besides . . ." His voice went soft, then collapsed into silence.

Duncan felt his face go red. It was hard to find the right words. But then maybe there were no right words. It was odd how easy it was to feel a prejudice. Much easier than trying to explain one. Maybe it was because when you tried to put your bitterness into words it didn't make sense. Maybe that was it.

"So you thought because I was a Campbell and a stranger in the glen—"

"I didn't think—" Duncan cut in angrily. By now his face felt as though it were on fire.

Campbell nodded. He said quietly. "That's the way it usually is, isn't it?" Suddenly he smiled. Duncan had never seen him smile. The jet black eyes in the lean face glowed. The teeth showed white and even.

"There were other things!" Duncan blustered, somehow feeling more foolish every minute. "Old Murdo saw you running outside Mordach Castle! Near where the wire had been rigged. Yes and at midnight it was too. No one in Kenmore goes near Mordach Castle at midnight."

"Somebody does," said young Campbell softly.

Duncan looked at him quickly. "What do you mean?"

Alan shrugged. "As you know, we live at the head of the glen. In a tent." He smiled sadly. "Like all the tinkers."

He paused, perhaps waiting for Duncan to make some comment. When Duncan was silent, he went on.

"Sometimes when everyone is sleeping, I sit outside the tent and look down at the glen. I like to sit and stare out into the night. Everything is different then. Why if you saw a man coming across towards you out of the shadows, you would not be knowing if he was a prince or a tinker. A MacDonald or a Campbell."

Duncan shifted uncomfortably. He wished that Uncle Alec were here. Uncle Alec knew how to deal with these things. "Go on."

"Well, twice when I was sitting looking out into the night, I saw a light from somewhere near Mordach Castle."

Duncan shrugged. "You have heard, of course, the old story about the castle? About it being haunted by the ghost of a young English girl named Mary Ellen? Many people say they have seen the light from her lantern."

"I know the old story," Alan said. "After all, Malcolm, the man she waited for, was a Campbell." He paused and looked away. "Only it was not just the steady beam from a lantern that I saw. There were other lights, too. Flashing lights. And they did not come just from the castle. They came from out at sea."

Duncan stared. "You mean someone on a ship was signaling to the castle?"

"I cannot prove it, of course. Yet what else could

it have been? Twice I saw them. The flashing lights and a smaller steady light that moved slowly around the castle."

"*Hmm.*" Now that was interesting. Why should anyone be sending signals from the castle to a ship offshore?" Duncan's brows furrowed. He suddenly looked curiously at the other. "By the way, I wondered why you never came into Kenmore?"

"And be treated like a tinker? A Gypsy? By everyone except the minister? He was the only one who came to see us." Alan shook his head emphatically. "No thank you. At least I'm as good as anyone when I am out in Glen Appin."

Duncan did not know where the words came from, but they were on his lips and he spoke them. "You're as good as anyone when you're in Kenmore, too." He paused, reddened, not quite sure of what he had just said. "I mean you've got as much right there as anyone else."

The tinker's dark eyes flashed mischievously. "Better, maybe. After all now, didn't this land belong once to the Clan Campbell?"

"That's old history," snapped Duncan. "Anyway, the land belongs to everyone now."

"Perhaps," Alan agreed mildly, "only I'm thinking that maybe somebody has my share. All I've got for myself is a few feet up at the head of the glen."

Duncan grinned in spite of himself. Fight it as he might, there was something likeable and friendly about this Alan Campbell. Of course, Uncle Alec would have said it was another Campbell trick. Only Uncle Alec wasn't here now. It was Uncle Alec, too, who had said it had been these same Campbells who had rigged up the wire by the castle. Duncan stiffened. But if it hadn't been the Campbells, then who had strung the wire across the narrow trail? It could only have been the way he had first figured. Whoever did it had a connection with the smuggling.

"That night," Duncan asked slowly, "when you were up near Mordach Castle, was there anything else you saw? I mean besides the lights?"

"Nothing." Young Campbell looked away sheepishly. "I'll have to say, though, I was just a bit nervous, being all by myself. Then I heard some kind of weird noise. Almost as though something was crying." He shivered. "That's when I went home. Running."

More than ever, Duncan felt himself drawn to the newcomer. Alan could have made an excuse for his hasty departure. Only he hadn't. Rather, he had admitted his fright. It was a fright that Duncan understood. He had been no less scared that night when he and Fiona had crossed the open field just below the rock. Of course Fiona being a girl—He stopped.

"Maybe if we went together—" he began, then bit back the rest of the words. It was crazy. Why only a few minutes ago, he had hated this tinker's son. He had been sure that it was this same Alan Campbell who had been responsible for his having finished last in the race. And now, just because he had met him and talked with him, he was suggesting they go up to Mordach Castle together. He would like to have recalled the words, but it was too late now. He could see the look on Alan Campbell's face, the look of excitement and surprise.

"You—you want me to go with you?" His eyes danced. "Why that would be grand! I know something is going on up there. I just know it."

"Of course, I'll have to wait until my ankle is a wee bit better," Duncan said stiffly. He was beginning to have regrets about the whole business. And just wait till Uncle Alec found out! Uncle Alec was not the sort that would be taken in by an open face and a friendly smile. Uncle Alec knew the value of being suspicious.

"Of course," agreed Alan quickly. "Can we say, two weeks from tonight? At ten? It should be dark then. I can meet you by that split oak tree on the other side of Loch Doune." He rubbed his hands together in anticipation. "It will be fine having someone along with me." He paused. "For a change."

Duncan felt it best to ignore the last comment. He looked down at his feet. "Tell me, that night you heard the noise, why now did you not go to the police? You felt something was going on. You had seen the lights. I think if it had been me, I would have gone straight to Constable Lindsay."

"And if I had been you, I would have done

the same. Only I'm not Duncan MacDonald. I'm Alan Campbell. I'm a stranger here. And I'm a tinker." He smiled. "I know fine how the police feel about tinkers and Gypsies. We're just riffraff. Thieves and worse. No I would not be caring to go with such stories to the police. The first thing they would ask would be what I was doing around the castle at midnight. And no matter what I said, I'm afraid they would not have believed me. I found out a long time ago that people believe only what they want to believe."

Duncan looked away quickly. What was there to say? Alan was right. Had he himself not been guilty of the same thing? He got to his feet. It was only when he had done so that he remembered his injured ankle. It was strange how in listening to the troubles of someone else, he had forgotten his own. He smiled wryly as he gingerly tested his foot. There would be lots of gossip around the village tonight about how he had finished last. And after all his brave talk about what a great runner he was. Well, let them gossip. He was still the best runner in Kenmore, even if no one but himself knew it.

"Two weeks then," he said. "I will be there. The split oak behind Loch Doune. At ten."

A smile touched the dark, serious face. "I will be there too," said Alan Campbell.

CHAPTER 14

A RAZOR-SHARP wind was blowing in from the Atlantic when Duncan stole out of the cottage. The sting in the air made him grateful for the heavy fisherman's jersey he had donned before leaving his room. He walked swiftly, pleased with the new feeling of strength in his right leg.

A thousand thoughts crowded his mind. What, if anything, would they find at the castle? What was the explanation of the noise that Alan Campbell had heard that night? Had the lights he had seen been the same lights that others had observed near Mordach Castle? Or was there more to it than that?

Duncan skirted wide around Loch Doune.

There was something menacing about the inky black waters. Something that chilled the blood and made the pulse beat faster. Old Murdo claimed there was no bottom to the lake, or at least no one had yet found any. Duncan could well believe it. When one cast a stone into Loch Doune, there was no pleasant splashing sound as in other lakes. There was only a hollow sigh as the stone vanished into the depths of the smooth black waters. Besides, there had been his own father—

Quite before he realized it, Duncan spotted a slender blackness loom out of the pale light on the far shore. It was the rendezvous point, the old oak tree, its base shattered long ago by a bolt of lightning. Duncan hesitated, then his quick eye caught the slim form of Alan Campbell emerge from the shadows under the tree.

They said little, each busy with his own thoughts, until they reached the border of the open stone field below the castle. Duncan gazed at it warily, recalling the last time he had ventured there with Fiona. He glanced apprehensively at the sliver of moon in the cloudless sky.

Alan must have caught his expression and read

his mind. The tinker's teeth gleamed in the half-light. "No, not that way," he whispered. "Follow me."

Duncan caught his arm. "But there is no other way directly up to Mordach Castle. You have to cross the field. It runs clear around to the precipice."

"At the edge of the cliff, there is a hidden path. It cannot be seen from below or above. That is how we shall go."

Duncan stared, suspicious for a reason he could not have explained. "Are you sure? No one in Kenmore knows of such a path."

"Don't forget that I am a tinker, and tinkers and the Gypsies know many things that others do not know." He paused. "Remember, too, that Mordach Castle belonged to the Chief of the Clan Campbell. You should not be surprised at all that we know its secrets better than others."

Duncan said no more, only grateful they would not have to cross the open field commanded by the grim castle. And Alan was right, of course, about the tinkers and Gypsies. They knew things that were never revealed to others. Their very way of life, drifting with the seasons through the Highlands and the Lowlands, led them to secrets that they shared only with members of their own groups. And, of course, Mordach Castle had been a stronghold of the Campbells. Any knowledge of a secret pathway would certainly have been known to the close members of the family.

His suspicions allayed but his curiosity aroused, Duncan followed his companion. Soon the castle was lost behind a lacy tangle of larches that struggled for roothold on the steep flinty hillside. The air was sharper now, keen with the salt bite of spindrift to it. The Atlantic. Already from somewhere to his left, Duncan's ears picked up the slow, steady boom of waves beating on rocks far below. Suddenly Alan came to a halt close to the edge of the cliff. Duncan felt the other's fingers tighten on his arm. "Did you hear something just now?"

"No, nothing. What—" Duncan never finished the sentence. At first, it had seemed just the movement of the wind in the trees. Only there were no trees where they were, just a few wind-whipped brambles and a stunted conifer. So the sound could not have been the wind stirring the leaves. If it had been a sound. Then, just when he had convinced himself that he had been mistaken, he heard it again. It came gently drifting down from the direction of the hidden castle, a small whimpering sound, half-human, half-animal. It died away in a soft little hiss of strangled air, as though a hand had suddenly jammed tight against a windpipe.

Duncan stood where he was, his skin prickled with a nameless fear. In the awful silence, he could hear the measured pounding of his heart under his wool jersey.

"That was the same sound I heard that night." Although Alan's voice seemed to break a little in his throat, it was steady enough. He withdrew his tensed fingers from Duncan's arm.

"The *same* sound?"

"Yes, listen. It is always the same."

Duncan listened. After a long silence it came again, just as it had before. The same eerie sob like a lost soul in pain. Then the soft, gurgling hiss of strangled air. Then the silence. Not a tremolo had varied. The same pitch. The same note of ascending doom. Then the final, interrupted gasp of air. Despite the fear that clung to him like a burr, Duncan's mind was remarkably lucid. He glanced at the phosphorescent hands of his watch. "You are right, Alan," he said thoughtfully. "It is always the same. And you say it was just like that when you were here that night?"

Alan nodded. He ran his tongue over his dry lips. "I will not soon forget it. I knew the stories, of course, that Mordach Castle was haunted. When I heard that noise I—I did not feel like going any farther. That was when Old Murdo must have seen me running. Somehow I just did not feel like staying where I was."

"I know what you mean," Duncan agreed soberly. He suddenly frowned. "There's something queer about this, though."

"You mean that sound? The fact that it never seems to change?"

"Right. And something else. The fact that there is an interval of exactly three minutes before it starts in again."

"So that was why you were looking at your watch. Well now and that is interesting, eh? If the sound does not change and everything about it is exactly the same, it can only mean one thing."

Duncan nodded. "A timed device of some kind. I'm sure of it."

"And so am I." Alan let his eyes travel up to the heights above him. "You are right. Something queer is going on." He hesitated for just a split second. "Well, there is one way to find out. Ready?"

Duncan hardly recognized the voice as his own. It seemed to come from miles away. "Ready."

Soundlessly, he crept after the shadowy form of young Campbell. They were almost at the edge of the precipice now, and the wind from the Atlantic was wet and raw, stinging his eyes. There was no sign of any trail, though, and he was just on the point of calling out that they were on the rim of the cliff when he saw it, a narrow path about two feet wide, winding up the black rock face. He swallowed. "That's the way?" he asked uneasily.

Again there was the sudden gleam of white teeth. "Do not worry, Duncan. It is safer than it looks. Besides it gets wider higher up."

Duncan nodded doubtfully, scarcely reassured. He did not like the way the narrow trail fell away into the darkness. The boom from the waves far below was louder now. Every instinct told him to stay

114

where he was. Yet he knew in his heart he could not turn back now. Not when he had come so far. And not in the presence of a Campbell. What Alan could do, he could do also. Grimly he scrambled onto the trail, steadied himself, then gingerly followed the other youth as he inched his way up the sheer face of the rock.

He pressed his body against the ice-cold wall and tried desperately to avert his eyes from the yawning abyss at the far edge of the path. There was a queer trembling in the muscles of his legs, and he fought hard against a feeling of nausea that threatened to engulf him at any moment. Slowly, foot by foot, he picked his way upwards until finally, as Alan had said, the trail suddenly widened. After that, it was a relatively simple scramble to the top of the rock wall.

Soundlessly, Alan pulled Duncan down into the coarse grass. With a sigh of relief, he eased his cramped legs. Only then did he notice that Alan was pointing at something straight ahead. Duncan lifted his eyes, then stared thunderstruck at the scene before him.

All his life he had seen Mordach Castle. Yet

never as he was seeing it now. Never this close. And from this angle. And at this hour. Silhouetted in stark relief against the moon, it swept upwards in a huge black cloud of scarred stone and mortar.

The parapets and rampart walks facing the west and the north had completely disappeared, but a good section of the nine-foot thick curtain wall used to defend the castle still stood intact. Most of the great central tower was also undamaged, although a number of the smaller surrounding turrets had sunk into heaps of rubble. Duncan stared, his eyes too small for the magnitude of the scene before him. There was something about Mordach Castle, something indescribably dark and evil that numbed the senses.

How long Duncan stared he would never know. There was something mesmerizing about the wall of tortured stone in front of him, something that held the eyes and would not let them go. Perhaps it was the moon behind the castle that accentuated the sheer blackness of the grim structure. The blackness was overwhelming, overpowering. Perhaps it was that. Perhaps—Duncan stared, his heart pounding. Could he have been mistaken? No, there it was again. Alan had seen it too, for his finger was pointing.

Pointing to a flicker of light from somewhere high in the great central tower.

The next second it was gone.

CHAPTER 15

AGAIN HE felt the pressure of Alan's fingers against his arm. He shifted his position slightly. Only then did he see what Alan was now looking at. A light blinking rapidly about two hundred yards offshore!

He did not have to be told what was happening. Someone in a ship out at sea was signaling to the central tower of Mordach Castle. Alan had been right after all. Right about the mysterious sounds he had heard. Right about the exchange of flashing lights. Only one point still remained unclear. The steady light that he claimed traveled slowly around the castle.

And then he saw it. A small square of light,

heaving gently in the darkness. The sort of light that a lantern might shed when swung loosely.

Duncan could feel his breath gather in a great lump in his throat as the wavering light advanced towards where they lay in the grass. Then suddenly a form materialized out of the blackness, a long hooded form, dressed in a white shroud. It seemed to float gently in the air, the soft beams from the swaying lantern casting darting tides of light over the shroud. Just as Duncan's blood turned to ice, he heard it. A low, keening sound like a soul in torment.

> *Is mor mo dhiobhail,*
> *Tha mi cianail.*
> *Fag leam fhin mi,*
> *Fag leam fhin mi.*

The specter passed only a few feet from where the two boys cowered in the long grass. In all his life, Duncan had never felt such fright. Ever since he was a child, he had heard the stories of the ghost of Mordach Castle. Now there it was, only a few feet away. Desperately, he tried to make himself as small as possible, praying the figure in white would not notice where they lay hidden. Then just when he felt his screaming nerves would snap under the strain, the swaying light passed them. Only the mournful notes—half croon, half sigh—still troubled the air. Duncan's mind, numb with fear as it was, automatically turned the words from the Gaelic into the more familiar English.

> *Great is my loss,*
> *I am sad.*
> *Leave me alone,*
> *Leave me alone.*

In a few moments the specter was gone, lost in sight behind the gateway in the massive eastern wall. High in the central tower, all was darkness. All was darkness, too, in the great sweep of the Atlantic. Everything was as it had been: the delicate turrets frosted with moonlight; the scent of the wet earth heavy in the night air; the melancholy boom of the waves from far below; the peevish murmur of the wind as it shuffled the leaves of a nearby rowan tree with quick deft fingers. Yes, everything was the same. Almost.

Gently Alan raised his head and studied the scene. Even in the half-light, Duncan could see the muscles still tight around the slightly frightened eyes. A faint tremor bent Alan's words when he spoke.

"You saw it, Duncan?"

"I did."

"The ghost of Mordach Castle. The one they call Mary Ellen."

"The same."

"That thing she was crooning in the Gaelic. Do you know what it was? I am not good at the Gaelic."

"It was a coronach, Alan. A lament for the dead."

Alan frowned. "Now that is strange, is it not? A lament for the dead?"

"And why should it be strange, Alan? Her Malcolm was dead."

"Yes, but Mary Ellen refused to believe it. As long as she lived alone in the castle, she was sure that one day he would return. Was that not the reason that every night, while she was alive, she lit her lantern to guide him home? No, Mary Ellen was *sure* that Malcom was not dead."

"That is true," Duncan agreed, wondering exactly what Alan was getting at.

"So if she believed he was not dead, why should she mourn for him? Yes and something else. Do they not say that poor Mary Ellen wore only her trousseau from that dark day when she returned to the castle until the day she died? She wanted to be ready for the wedding." Alan spoke softly, deliberately. "But who gets married in a shroud?"

Duncan nodded. "That is also true." He stared up at the black outline of the castle, conscious of a vague unrest. There was something wrong somewhere. Something— He stopped and recollection came stabbing into his mind. His eyes were snapping when he turned to Alan. "There is something else. Something I had not thought of before."

"And what is that?"

"Just this," Duncan said grimly, "why should Mary Ellen's ghost be speaking Gaelic? You will remember that she was English. I'm certain there were few words she could speak in the old tongue. So if it wasn't the ghost of Mary Ellen who just passed here, then it could only be "

He never finished the sentence, for at that moment Alan reached out and with a muffled ejaculation, thrust him down into the grass. Then suddenly Duncan heard the scrape of a shoe from somewhere just behind them. He caught a glimpse of a figure stealing out of the shadows near the castle. Then a cautious voice came up from below the rim of the cliff.

"Ned?"

There was a grunt. "Who were you expecting, Lady Macbeth? But I'm warning you, Dave Cummings. One more week of this ghost walking business, and I'll go out of my mind. This place is starting to give *me* the creeps. I could have sworn I saw something a little while ago. Just when I was making the rounds with my lantern."

The man called Dave muttered something under his breath as he pulled himself up over the cliff edge. "This is the last haul of watches and diamonds, remember? You said we should pull out after tonight. This place is getting too hot, Ned." He peered around uneasily. "You don't think it was your nerves before? I mean about seeing something?"

Ned, still in the long shroud he had worn when he made his circuit of the castle, nodded his head

123

glumly. "Guess maybe it was nerves. I'm getting awfully jumpy lately. Living in this old dump and going around singing nutty songs in Gaelic to myself. Somehow I've got an idea there's only one idiot I'm scaring with all this crazy ghost business. Poor Ned Turner himself."

Cummings shrugged. "Harry said he'd stand by out there. He'll be sending a boat to pick us up around midnight. Then all our worries are over. The car from Glasgow with Joe and Sam will be along in an hour or so. They'll pick up this stuff. After that, it's good-bye Mordach Castle, hello Piccadilly for all of us. Why—"

He stopped abruptly. Both smugglers were staring. Staring in the direction of the small stone that Duncan had dislodged with his cramped foot and which was now clattering down the steep slope.

"What was that?" It was Ned Turner who spoke. His eyes squinted nervously into the darkness where the boys lay breathless in the grass.

The second smuggler rose silently to his feet. There was a muscular maturity to him, but he moved cat-quick and he crouched warily as he advanced.

"I don't know," he said softly. The moon caught the blue-white flash of steel in his hand. "But I'm sure aiming to find out."

CHAPTER 16

THERE WAS just one thing to do. Instinctively, both boys did it. As though released from a tightly compressed spring, Alan flung himself forward and seized Dave Cummings around the ankles. At the same moment, Duncan, aiming higher, brought his shoulder into violent collision with the smuggler's stomach. With a howl of pain and wrath, Cummings went crashing backwards into his companion. Ned Turner, still wrapped in his shroud, let out an unghostlike bellow as he landed hard on the equally hard ground.

Taking advantage of the confusion, Duncan and Alan wasted not a second in scrambling to their feet.

"Quick, Alan! The castle!" cried Duncan as he sprinted over the open ground towards the west wall. They had been lucky in having been able to take the smugglers by surprise. They could not hope to be so fortunate again. Both men were powerfully built, and almost certainly it would go badly for the boys should they be overtaken.

Alan needed no second urging. He was off like a shot, one step behind Duncan, his head low, his legs churning. The boys were a good fifteen yards away before the smugglers, recovering from the attack, were able to struggle to their feet and take up the pursuit.

Darting into the shadows, the boys squirmed through a ragged gap in the towering wall at the same moment. Once on the other side, they found themselves in the courtyard of the castle, a rectangular wilderness, nettle-choked and littered with crumbled stone and debris. With pounding hearts, in the pale light of the crescent moon, they looked swiftly around them. There was only one place that looked as though it might offer some measure of sanctuary. The great central tower. Both youths saw it at the same time. Without a word they were off, stumbling over the treacherous ground between them and the tower. Behind him, Duncan could hear the shouts of the two smugglers. Because of their familiarity with the rough terrain, the men were beginning to close the gap dangerously.

Tugging frantically, the boys succeeded in thrusting back the great wooden door of the tower. They rushed down a low corridor. All at once, a damp, musty smell assailed Duncan's nostrils. He took a few more steps, hesitated, then stopped. He turned, and in the darkness something cold and hard brushed against his hand. He drew himself back sharply before he realized what he had touched. An iron chain. They were in the dungeon of the castle.

"I saw them, Ned! This way!" a voice cried out triumphantly from somewhere behind them. Duncan's eyes, quick with urgency, probed the blackness of the prison. Alongside him, he could hear Alan's breathing. They were caught. Trapped. As trapped as any of the poor wretches who had been thrown here to die three hundred years ago.

Duncan threw out his arm in a gesture of despair. His heart seemed to skip a beat. Had he been mistaken? No! It was not the rough stone of the dungeon walls that his fingers were touching. It was a smooth piece of wood. A heavy, horizontal beam. It could only be one thing. The crossbar of a door. With a quick heave, he raised it and swung it open. With Alan at his heels, he darted up a series of long flights of uneven sandstone steps until they finally burst out onto the parapet.

Duncan's heart sank like a stone as his eyes swept the gabled enclosure of the turret. What a fool he had been. He should have known there would be no way out other than by the spiral stairway that they had just climbed. They were caught, with no hope of escape. It would be only a matter of moments before the smugglers found the dungeon empty and guessed they had taken the stairway to the turret. Then it would be all over for both of them.

It was the cool, resourceful mind of Alan Campbell that sensed the chance, the only chance. With a bound, he pulled his supple body through an opening in the low stone wall. "The ivy!" he cried. "Quick! It's our only chance!"

His knees weak as water, his hands trembling, Duncan followed the other over the wall. It was hardly a question of wanting to go. There was no choice. That is if he wanted to stay out of the hands of the two furious smugglers. And unappealing as it might be to hang suspended in the darkness from the heights of Mordach Castle, it was no less unappealing than facing the menace of the desperadoes.

The wind whistled around his ears as, with fear-frozen fingers, Duncan clung to the tough vine for dear life. Finally, convinced that he was not going to drop the one hundred feet to the courtyard—at least not yet—he gingerly let himself down, first the one hand, then the other. Once a clump of ivy root came away sickeningly in his grasp. Only a quick lunge by Alan braced him against the tower until his fingers found a new hold. Finally, after what seemed an eternity, his feet touched the hard stone of the courtyard. He could have fainted with relief.

"The door to the dungeon," panted Alan. "Hurry! Before they get to the bottom of the stairs!"

His head still spinning, his arms aching in their sockets, Duncan leaped after Alan. There was hardly a moment to spare. Already the smugglers, realizing that the ivy might not hold their greater weight, were thundering down the spiral stairway.

The boys raced through the open tower gate together. Wasting not a second, they groped their way through the midnight blackness of the narrow corridor until it widened into the dungeon. Neither Duncan nor Alan had to be told where the stairs to the tower were. Their ears were filled with the clamor of their pursuers as the smugglers rushed headlong down the circular steps.

The men could have been no more than a dozen steps away when the boys found the great wooden door and swung it closed. "Quick!" panted Duncan. His shoulder crashed hard against the door, "The crossbar!" His hand flailed the blackness for the heavy bar. It was gone. Then a quick shout of triumph struck his ears, and the next moment Alan had dropped the crossbar in place. And not a second too soon. The door had scarcely been secured when the two smugglers reached it. A baffled roar came from the other side as the pursuers pounded on the stout oak.

Losing not a second, the boys retreated swiftly from the dungeon, the shouts and threats of the trapped men loud in their ears. Only when they had emerged from the tower itself did Duncan halt and heave a long sigh of relief.

"Close," he muttered, looking back over his shoulder into the darkness. "Never thought we were going to make it, Alan."

"We haven't made it yet," returned the other. "Remember what the man named Dave said? There would be a car coming along in an hour or so to pick up the stuff. After that, a boat would be put ashore to collect our two friends. One of us will have to stay here to keep an eye on things. The other will go for help." He paused and said deliberately. "It is better that I stay."

Duncan looked around doubtfully. In addition to the sinister atmosphere of the place itself, it would not be pleasant for the one who stayed behind in the courtyard of Mordach Castle. Who knew how long the wooden door would withstand the pounding of the smugglers; or whether they might not retreat to the tower and take a chance on the ivy?

"And why now should the risk be yours, Alan?" he demanded. "It is you who will return for help and I who will stay."

"If I ask you a fair question, will you promise to give me a fair answer?"

Duncan frowned. What was Alan getting at? "I will."

"Who in your honest opinion, Duncan Mac-Donald, is the fastest runner in Kenmore?"

Duncan's chin jutted out. "I am!" he exclaimed fiercely. "And I don't care who knows it."

Alan grinned. "Then doesn't it make sense that you run for help while I stay here?"

Duncan glowered. He had been trapped by his pride.

"You *are* the fastest runner. Many a time I have lain hidden in the glen and watched you. That is why I spoke to you after the race. I know you should have won. There is none swifter of foot in all the length of Glen Appin than you, Duncan. So hurry now, for there's not a moment to lose."

Grateful for the words, Duncan turned to go. He glanced back over his shoulder at the gloomy tower that had seen so much of bloodshed and death—and might see more. Alan was right. There wasn't a moment to lose. The messengers from

Glasgow might be arriving anytime. Or the smugglers might succeed in breaking free from the tower. Already the door seemed to be groaning under their unremitting assault. There was no saying how long it could hold.

"I won't be long, Alan," he promised. "I'll get Constable Lindsay and some of the men." He paused. "Just stay out of trouble," he added anxiously.

Alan's low chuckle came from somewhere in the darkness. The battering at the dungeon door was louder. More insistent. More ominous. "I'll do my best, Duncan. You do yours."

CHAPTER 17

AND NOW, surely, he was a swift-footed courier, bearings the news as in the old days of the clans. True, he bore no fiery brand in his hand. Still, was he not the fastest runner, and did he not bear news? Yes, and exciting news. Had not the whole country been aroused about the smuggling that had been going on all summer? Had not the government itself sent its agents up and down the Hebrides and the West Coast in search of the elusive gang? But it had been Alan and he who had caught them. Or would, he reminded himself grimly, if he were able to get back to Mordach Castle in time with reinforcements.

As he did not have to fear about being seen from

the tower, he took the familiar trail that led down to the open field of scree and rubble. He could use his fleetness of foot here to better advantage than would be possible if he tried to negotiate the secret path down the cliff face. Besides, there was too great a chance of a misstep in the dangerous route that the Campbells had used long ago to slip out of their castle. And one misstep in the darkness high above the jagged black rocks would be the last step he would ever take.

He had never run before with such power. Perhaps because he had never before run with such purpose. His feet fairly skimmed across the heather. And now Loch Doune, moon-misted, was in view and the great sweep of the glen. With the more even footing, he increased his speed, spurred by the mental picture of Alan, alone in the darkened courtyard of sinister Mordach Castle. Perhaps even now the smugglers had escaped from the tower and found him. Perhaps the messengers from Glasgow had arrived early. Perhaps—

Duncan jerked his head angrily as though to shake loose the unpleasant thoughts. There was only one thing to think about, only one thing to do: to get to Kenmore as quickly as his feet could carry him.

The terrific pace he had set for himself began to take its toll. His muscles began to ache with every forward thrust of his legs. But now he could see the small twinkling lights of the village. Grimly, he drove himself forward, draining from his exhausted body the final measure of effort. Then suddenly, he felt the smoothness of pavement under his feet, and he was on High Street. It was only a matter of moments after that that he was gasping out his story in the warmth of Constable Lindsay's home.

Constable John Lindsay represented in his person the entire police force of Kenmore. As there was scarcely any crime, there was little for the constable to do. John Lindsay was a sleepy-eyed, deliberate-moving man, a little too solid of jowl and middle. Yet when he wanted to, John Lindsay could be brisk and fast moving. Like now. He wasted not a moment. While Duncan gratefully gulped down a mug of sweet, hot tea, the policeman was on the phone, barking out instructions with swiftness and authority.

Duncan blinked. He had never seen Constable

Lindsay in this role before. He was surprised, too, to note that the policeman must have prepared himself for just such a situation as this. A situation where, as the sole representative of law and order, he would need civilian help. By the time Duncan had left the cozy kitchen and squeezed himself into the front seat of the Land Rover, several ancient cars crammed with villagers were converging on them from all directions.

Duncan's spirits soared when he saw the force gathered around the constable getting instructions. There was Dan Chisholm, the big blacksmith; Malcolm Duncan, the powerfully built fisherman; Gavin Brown, cat-quick and muscle-ridged, who had been a commando in the army. And why there was Mr. Cameron. What could have brought him out? With a stout wooden club no less. And wasn't that Old Murdo over there? Murdo didn't have a weapon like any of the other men, although he had his fiddle. Still, if one flinched at the queer noises when Old Murdo played, one might call the fiddle a weapon at that!

But it was when Uncle Alec clambered into the back seat of the Land Rover, his great sword wob-

bling dangerously over his head, that Duncan really gasped in astonishment. And a moment after Uncle Alec got in, down the street came fat Wullie, his tongue lolling as he lumbered towards them. With a sigh of relief, the big dog heaved himself in, then plopped down on Duncan's aching feet like a small cow.

"Uncle Alec!" the boy exclaimed as the car shot off with a roar, "what are you doing here?"

"Campbells!" thundered the fiery little man. "They're back! Up at Mordach Castle!"

The minister, seated alongside him in the bouncing car, smiled in the darkness. "Smugglers, Mr. MacDonald," he corrected gently. "The only Campbell in Mordach Castle is the brave young lad who went up there with Duncan and is still up there." He paused as though realizing the futility of reasoning with Uncle Alec, who sat with raised sword, his eyes glowering with excitement. "Why don't you try to explain to him, Duncan? Besides I'm anxious to hear your story myself."

As the stout little car negotiated the rough terrain, Duncan, hanging on for dear life, brought the men up to date on everything that had happened.

Only when he had finished did Uncle Alec slowly lower his sword. He was silent for a long moment, staring out into the emptiness of Glen Appin. When he spoke, it was softly, as though to himself. "It's hard to believe after all these years that we are on the same side, the Campbells and the MacDonalds. Well, well. I'll have to think about that."

CHAPTER 18

LEAVING THE cars at the foot of the steep incline to the castle, Constable Lindsay deployed his force with no waste motions. His voice was cool and matter-of-fact, as though storming castles at midnight was something he did every day. Watching him, Duncan could scarcely believe he was the same sleepy individual he and everyone in Kenmore knew as the slowest moving police officer in all the Highlands. There was a small joke among the villagers that the constable was so lazy he wouldn't walk down High Street unless the wind was blowing from the right direction. There was nothing lazy about him now. It only went to show how events and challenges sometimes changed people and brought out all that was best in them.

"You, Mr. Cameron, will take three men and proceed up the north flank. You, Gavin, will take another three men by the south flank. Duncan here tells me there's a secret path up the cliff face. He and I and you, Dan Chisholm, will go by that route. I don't want too many there in case the men from the ship offshore should decide to land a party. The rest of you will be under Malcolm Duncan. You will approach the castle from the east. And all of you be on the alert for young Campbell. We want to be certain he doesn't get hurt should there be a fight. Any questions so far?"

Davie Thomson, the postman, shifted uneasily and cocked a wary eye at the grim silhouette of the castle high above. "They say there's a real ghost up there," he said.

Constable John Lindsay did not laugh often. He did not laugh now. Only his lips bent in what might have been a smile. "The real ghost is on our side," he returned drily. "And now if there are no further questions, we'll synchronize our watches. In exactly twenty minutes, I'll blow this whistle. That will be the signal for everyone to rush into the castle. Remember, we don't know how many may be there by this time. If our surprise works, however, we should take the lot of them." He nodded brusquely. "Good luck."

Within a matter of seconds they were gone, swallowed up in the shadows. Duncan, his heart beating just a little too fast, led Constable Lindsay and the big blacksmith towards the secret path. The wind had shifted, and the boy felt a drift of quick rain against his face as he cautiously led the way up the rock face. It was cold now. Much colder. Once Duncan dared to take his eyes from the narrow path and look out into the great sweep of the sea. Just as he did so, a light flashed from somewhere in the great black emptiness. The next moment it was gone.

So they were out there still. Perhaps they already suspected that something had gone wrong. Perhaps they were sending reinforcements ashore now. Grimly the boy dismissed the thoughts that nagged him. No sense in thinking of anything but the winding path under his feet. One false step in the darkness and it would be all over. Then quite before he realized it, they reached the point where the trail widened. He breathed easier. In a matter of moments, they had pulled themselves over the rim of the precipice. Crouched low, they hurried through a tangle of waist-high bracken until they drew near to the ruins of the great west wall. Satisfied they had not been seen, Constable Lindsay eased himself down onto the ground, one leg drawn under his body. Wordlessly, Duncan and the blacksmith sank down beside him.

The policeman cupped his fingers and studied his watch. "We have five minutes," he whispered.

In all his life, Duncan had never seen time pass so slowly. The ground seemed to press upwards against his chest so that it was hard to breathe. His eyes never left the outlines of the great wall. Behind it Alan was waiting. Or should be if everything had gone all right. If he had not been found. A cold sweat broke out on the palms of his hands. Everything *had* to be all right.

Suddenly from somewhere in the courtyard behind the wall, Duncan heard the voice, cold with menace. "Answer me, boy, or it's a knife you'll be getting between those ribs of yours. Who sent you up here to spy?"

"No one." It was Alan's voice, a little frightened but steady enough.

"No one, eh? Good thing that Harry and the boys came over from the boat to find out what was wrong. Got you good and proper they did, sneaking around on your hands and knees. It's the knife for you, boy, or the cliff if you don't find a quick tongue in your head. So I'm asking you again. What were you doing here? You and that other one who got away?"

"I—we—we heard about the ghost. The ghost of Mary Ellen that's supposed to haunt Mordach Castle."

"Look!" snapped another voice, a voice Duncan did not recognize, "Sam and I have to get back to Glasgow with the stuff. You said it would be the last haul anyway, Ned. You settle this business. After all, you don't need seven of us to take care of this little punk, do you?"

Duncan felt his blood run cold as he heard the threats. He wheeled around to the constable, whose body was bent forward, his eyes on the green phosphorescent hand as it swept around his watch. Without taking his eyes from the watch, John Lindsay thrust a police whistle between his lips. Then suddenly there was a long, shrill *wheep*. It was followed a split second later by a series of wild yells as the attackers converged on the castle from all sides.

As he charged towards the gap in the wall, Duncan could hear a weird scraping noise, like a ghost in pain. Then he remembered. Old Murdo! With his fiddle substituting for the bagpipe that had always led the Highlanders into battle in the past, Old Murdo was inspiring the men forward.

After a few minutes of fierce give and take, it was all over. It would have been difficult to give the reason for the smugglers' sudden loss of heart in the fight. Perhaps it had been the surprise of the attack and the vigor with which it had been carried out. Or again it might have been the unnerving sound of Old Murdo's fiddle. Then it could have been the sight of big Wullie padding forward in the moonlight, looking like a great silver wolf on the prowl. Whatever the reason, there was no doubt as to the outcome after the men of Kenmore had swarmed over the smugglers.

"Alan!" cried Duncan looking around wildly. "Alan! Are you all right?"

"Just grand!" hailed a cheery voice from the shadows of the courtyard. The next moment the tinker's son stepped into view. He grinned when he saw Duncan. "You see, I was right, wasn't I? You are the fastest runner in Kenmore. I could hardly believe it when I heard that whistle. I'll admit, though, I was a wee bit worried for a moment or so."

"So was I," confessed Duncan. His eyes swept over the disgruntled desperadoes. He had never seen such a woebegone crew in his life. The two men who had arrived by car were rubbing assorted injuries and muttering. The three others who had put ashore from the ship and had surprised Alan were moaning softly and cradling their bruised heads between their hands. The two smugglers who Duncan and Alan had clashed with were sitting apart from the others. Their faces were twisted with hate as they glared at the two boys. Ned Turner was still in his long shroud, his face white, his eyes bulging. He looked like a ghost who had just seen a ghost.

Old Murdo joined the boys. He jerked a thumb at unhappy Ned Turner. "Got the poor soul with this," he exclaimed as he indicated his battered fiddle. He stared dolefully at his instrument. *"Och* and I'll never forgive myself if I broke it. He's got an awfully hard head on him, the man has."

The Reverend Mr. Cameron smiled. He appeared to be enjoying himself. "So you see, Murdo, music does soothe the savage beast after all," he remarked with a chuckle. He suddenly looked down at his watch and frowned. *"That* late? Well, I think it's been quite an evening for everyone." He flicked a sidelong glance at the boys. "Especially for you two youngsters."

"But I'm not tired at all," protested Duncan in dismay. "It's early."

"That's what I mean. Early. In the morning. Now off with you both. You'll have plenty to talk about tomorrow."

"But what about the rest of them out in the boat?" Alan asked. "They're sure to get away."

Constable Lindsay snapped the handcuffs around Turner's wrists. He shook his head. "I don't think so, Alan. I put a call through from Kenmore. There should be a police launch out there any minute."

Uncle Alec peered around, then stared up at the dark tower. He looked disappointed, his big broadsword clasped in his two hands. "Maybe there are some hiding in the castle," he suggested hopefully.

"I'm afraid not," said the policeman. "This is the lot." He nudged Ned Turner forward. "On your way."

One by one the bruised and dejected smugglers, bound securely and closely guarded by the villagers, started on their way down the mountain. Ned led the sad procession, perhaps because he looked the saddest in his burial robes. After he had proceeded some little way from the castle, he suddenly paused and wheeled around. His long face was full of venom as he glared back at the castle. "I hope I never see that dump again," he exclaimed with disgust.

It was Constable Lindsay, though, who had the last word.

"I think that can be arranged, Ned," he said. "Just mention it to the judge."

CHAPTER 19

"IT WAS all very clever," said Constable Lindsay two days later as a group of the villagers sat around the dinner table in the MacDonald home. "Ned Turner and his friends had heard the old stories about Mordach Castle and the ghost of Mary Ellen. They knew that most everyone in Kenmore had a healthy dread of the place. Overlooking the Atlantic as it did, and hidden away from the busier ports, it was an ideal spot to land contraband. And, of course, once landed and stored in the castle, it was a simple matter to get it down to the Glasgow road. Yes, it was all very clever. Only it wasn't quite clever enough, thanks to our two young friends here."

151

Duncan felt his face burn as every eye turned approvingly toward where the two boys sat together. Ever since the happenings of two nights ago, there had been only one subject of conversation the whole length of Glen Appin—the battle with the smugglers in Mordach Castle. Why the local newspaper itself, the *Kenmore Press,* had sent a photographer to his house to take his picture. There was even talk that the Edinburgh and Glasgow newspapers were sending reporters to Kenmore for on-the-spot stories. Oh, and everything had been thrilling and wonderful. There had been only one sour note. That had taken place when Fiona had slyly kissed him just as the photographer was about to take his picture. It was a fair disgrace the way some girls behaved these days.

The Reverend Mr. Cameron nodded as he helped himself to a bannock and cheese. "It was clever, too, the way the gang hooked up those hidden microphones to scare off anyone who ventured near the castle. And of course behind all the microphones and the trip wires that signaled when anyone was approaching was the fearsome ghost of Mordach Castle itself, in the person of Ned Turner."

He smiled. "I'm afraid the only place our friend will be haunting for the next few years will be the inside of a prison."

"And that goes for the rest of them," added Constable Lindsay. "There were two more of them on the boat. Nine altogether." The fixed lines on his dour face moved over to accommodate the makings of a smile. "I never dreamed smuggling was so popular."

Dan Chisholm poured himself a cup of strong tea. "I'm thinking it won't be so popular as it was," he observed drily. He turned to Uncle Alec. "Right, Alec?"

Duncan's uncle nodded. The old gentleman had been unusually silent during the meal. In fact he had been unusually silent ever since the events at Mordach Castle. It was not like Uncle Alec to be silent. Whatever was on his mind was usually on his tongue. Still, there it was. The little man with the fierce moustache and the equally fierce temper seemed different. For what reason, though, Duncan could only guess.

"Aye, Dan, it's right you are," Uncle Alec said. His gaze was empty, as though his thoughts were elsewhere. Finally, he swallowed hard and seemed to come to a decision. Slowly he turned and fixed his eyes on Alan. "I have something I must tell you, lad. Something that will not be easy for me to say at all. Yet something that must be said."

Alan regarded him warily, the old caution in his eyes. He did not speak.

"I have been thinking much these past few days. Thinking how all my life has been spent brooding over things that happened long ago. Feeling sorry for the poor MacDonalds and all they had suffered at the hands of the Campbells." He stopped, waiting for the words to come. The words that had taken a lifetime to come. The words so strange and clumsy against his tongue. So difficult to speak.

"The other night, after everyone had left the courtyard, I stood for a while in the loneliness of what was left of Mordach Castle. I thought how this had once been the great house of the chief of Clan Campbell. Then the enemies of the Campbells had fallen on it and put to the sword those who had desperately defended it. And who had done this deed? The MacDonalds, my own people."

Alan sat forward in his chair, his face rigid, his fingers clasped.

"I thought, standing there in the awful stillness, how easy it is to remember the sorrow that others bring to us, and how easy to forget the sorrow we often bring to others." He turned his head and was silent for a moment. "I'm minding, too, something from the Bible. Something about how hate begets hate, and there is no end to it at all, at all. So Alan Campbell, friend of my nephew Duncan, and my friend, too, I bid you welcome to the house of the MacDonalds. It is your house, although a poor one indeed beside the one you had at Mordach Castle. And here's my hand upon it."

There was a loud burst of applause as Alan, a little shyly, pushed back his chair and extended his hand first to Uncle Alec, then with a grin to Duncan.

Old Murdo winked at Alan after the boy had resumed his seat. "Just you mind and don't bring that ghost with you when you come here, Alan Campbell. One haunted house in Kenmore is enough, just." He reached for his fiddle. "And now

I think it's time we had a wee tune." He scratched his bow across the strings of his ancient fiddle. "And would there be any special requests?" he asked.

Fiona frowned. *"Mm,* let me think. You wouldn't know 'Annie Laurie' now would you, Murdo?" she asked, poker faced.

" 'Annie Laurie'? Why and that's the one I like best, too, Fiona." With a flourish, he withdrew a polka-dotted handkerchief from his pocket and crammed it under his tilted chin. Positioning the violin, he plucked at the strings, then closed his eyes and raised his bow. No one moved until the last sad notes had expired on the quivering strings. Then everyone cheered. Whether at the way Old Murdo had played or because he had stopped playing, Duncan was not sure.

A shaft of sunlight fell across the floor, and Duncan's eyes idly followed it to the window. Then he saw it, far away, across the broad purple sweep of Glen Appin—the great heap of crumbling stone that had been the proud home of the Campbells. Only somehow it didn't look as grim and fearsome as he had always remembered it, now that its ghost was gone.

Perhaps, he mused, it was the same with the old stories of the old days that Uncle Alec had just been speaking about. The old stories that had inspired so much fear and misunderstanding. They had a ghost too, like the ghost of Mordach Castle. A ghost forever wailing of old wrongs. And once that ghost was routed, why everything looked different. Just as now, Mordach Castle looked different, standing like a giant oak tree, proud against the sun.

Duncan nodded to himself, sure in his heart he was right. After all was said and done, it was just a question of how you looked at things—and people.

No more than that.

ABOUT THE AUTHOR

William MacKellar was born in Glasgow, Scotland and came to the United States at the age of eleven. He attended New York University and the University of Geneva, Switzerland.

He has published many children's books in addition to *Mound Menace* and *Mystery of Mordach Castle* for Follett.

Mr. MacKellar, his wife, and their three children make their home in West Hartford, Connecticut.